TOM
SAWYER

—— **Mark Twain** ——

TOM
SAWYER

PETER HADDOCK PUBLISHING

Published in this edition 1997 by Peter Haddock Publishing,
United Kingdom
Reprinted 1999, 2004

© 1997 This arrangement, text and illustrations,
Geddes & Grosset, David Dale House,
New Lanark, Scotland

© Original text John Kennett

Illustrated by Jane Swift (Simon Girling Associates)

ISBN 0 7105 0931 6

Printed and bound in Poland

Contents

To the Reader

I am sure you will have seen a film, or watched a programme on TV, that has been made from some famous book. If you enjoyed the film or programme, you may have decided to read the book.

Then what happens? You get the book and, it's more than likely, you get a shock as well! You turn ten or twenty pages, and nothing seems to *happen*. Where are all the lively people and exciting incidents? When, you say, will the author get down to telling the story? In the end you will probably throw the book aside and give it up. Now, why is that?

Well, perhaps the author was writing for adults and not for children. Perhaps the book was written a long time ago, when people had more time for reading and liked nothing better than a book that would keep them entertained for weeks.

We think differently today. That's why I've taken some of these wonderful books, and retold them for you. If you enjoy them in this shorter form, then I hope that when you are older you will go back to the original books, and enjoy all the more the wonderful stories they have to tell.

About the Author

Mark Twain was the pen-name of the American author, Samuel Langhorne Clemens, who was born in Florida, Missouri, in 1835 and died in 1910. He tried many jobs before becoming a writer: he was printer, river-pilot, journalist, gold miner and prospector in turn.

Mark Twain wrote many books, but perhaps the most popular and best known are *Tom Sawyer* and *Huckleberry Finn*, the book about the adventures of Tom's best friend.

Chapter One
Tom and Aunt Polly

"Tom!"

No answer.

"Tom!"

No answer.

"What's gone with that boy, I wonder? You Tom!"

The old lady pulled her spectacles down and looked over them, about the room; then she put them up and looked out under them. She seldom or never looked *through* them for so small a thing as a boy, for they were her state pair, the pride of her heart, and were built for "style" not service; she could have seen through a pair of stove lids as well. She looked perplexed a moment and said, not fiercely, but still loud enough for the furniture to hear, "Well, I lay if I get hold of you, I'll——"

She did not finish, for by this time she was bending down and punching under the bed with the broom—and so she needed breath to punctuate the punches with. She resurrected nothing but the cat.

"I never did see the beat of that boy!"

She went to the open door and stood in it, and looked out among the tomato vines and "jimpson" weeds that constituted the garden. No Tom. So she lifted up her voice, at an angle calculated for distance, and shouted.

"Y-o-u-u Tom!"

There was a slight noise behind her, and she turned just in

time to seize a small boy by the slack of his roundabout and arrest his flight." There! I might 'a thought of that closet. What you been doing in there?"

"Nothing."

"Nothing! Look at your hands, and look at your mouth. What *is* that truck?"

"*I* don't know, aunt."

"Well, *I* know. It's jam, that's what it is. Forty times I've said if you didn't let that jam alone I'd skin you. Hand me that switch."

The switch hovered in the air. The peril was desperate.

"My! Look behind you, aunt!"

The old lady whirled around and snatched her skirts out of danger, and the lad fled, on the instant, scrambled up the high board fence, and disappeared over it. His aunt Polly stood surprised a moment, and then broke into a gentle laugh.

"Hang the boy! Can't I never learn anything? Ain't he played me tricks enough like that for me to be looking out for him by this time? But old fools is the biggest fool there is. Can't learn any old dog new tricks, as the saying is. But, my goodness, he never plays them alike two days, and how is a body to know what's coming? He 'pears to know just how long he can torment me before I get my dander up, and he knows if he can make out to put me off for a minute, or make me laugh, it's all down again, and I can't hit him a lick. I ain't doing my duty by that boy, and that's the Lord's truth, goodness knows. Spare the rod and spile the child, as the good book says. I'm a laying up sin and suffering for us both, *I* know. He's full of the old scratch, but laws-a-me! He's my own dead sister's boy, poor thing, and I ain't got the heart to lash him, somehow. Every time I let him off my conscience does hurt me so; and every time I hit him my

old heart most breaks. Well-a-well, man that is born of a woman is of few days and full of trouble, as the Scripture says, and I reckon it's so. He'll play hookey this afternoon and I'll just be obliged to make him work tomorrow, to punish him. It's mighty hard to make him work Saturdays, when all the boys is having a holiday, but he hates work more than he hates anything else, and I've got to do some of my duty by him, or I'll be the ruination of the child."

Tom did play hookey, and he had a very good time. He got back home barely in time to help Jim, the small coloured boy, saw next day's wood, and split the kindlings before supper—at least he was there in time to tell his adventures to Jim, while Jim did three-fourths of the work. Tom's younger brother (or rather half-brother), Sid, was already through with his part of the work (picking up chips), for he was a quiet boy, and had no adventurous, troublesome ways.

While Tom was eating his supper and stealing sugar as opportunity offered, Aunt Polly asked him questions that were full of guile, and very deep—for she wanted to trap him into damaging revealments. Like many other simple-hearted souls, it was her pet vanity to believe she was endowed with a talent for dark and mysterious diplomacy, and she loved to contemplate her most transparent devices as marvels of low cunning. Said she, "Tom, it was middling warm in school, warn't it?"

"Yes, 'm."

"Powerful warm, warn't it?"

"Yes, 'm."

"Didn't you want to go in a-swimming, Tom?" A bit of a scare shot through Tom—a touch of uncomfortable suspicion. He searched Aunt Polly's face, but it told him nothing. So he said:

"No, 'm—well, not very much."

The old lady reached out her hand and felt Tom's shirt, and said:

"But you ain't too warm now, though."

And it flattered her to reflect that she had discovered that the shirt was dry without anybody knowing that that was what she had in her mind. But in spite of her Tom knew where the wind lay now. So he forestalled what might be the next move.

"Some of us pumped on our heads—mine's damp yet. See?"

Aunt Polly was vexed to think she had overlooked that bit of circumstantial evidence and missed a trick. Then she had a new inspiration:

"Tom, you didn't have to undo your shirt collar where I sewed it to pump on your head, did you? Unbutton your jacket!"

The trouble vanished out of Tom's face. He opened his jacket. His shirt collar was securely sewed.

"Bother! Well, go 'long with you. I made sure you'd played hookey and been a-swimming. But I forgive ye, Tom, I reckon you're a kind of a singed cat, as the saying is—better 'n you look. *This* time."

She was half sorry her sagacity had miscarried, and half glad that Tom had stumbled into obedient conduct for once.

But Sidney said:

"Well, now, if I didn't think you sewed his collar with white thread, but it's black."

"Why, I did sew it with white! Tom!"

But Tom did not wait for the rest. As he went out of the door, he said:

"Siddy, I'll lick you for that."

In a safe place Tom examined two large needles which were

thrust into the lapels of his jacket— and had thread bound about them—one needle carried white thread and the other black. He said:

"She'd never noticed if it hadn't been for Sid. Confound it, sometimes she sews it with white and sometimes she sews it with black. I wish to geeminy she'd stick to one or t'other—I can't keep the run of 'em. But I bet you I'll get Sid for that. If I don't, blame my cats."

He was not the model boy of the village. He knew the model boy very well, though, and loathed him.

Within two minutes, or even less, he had forgotten all his troubles. Not because his troubles were one whit less heavy and bitter to him than a man's are to a man, but because a new and powerful interest bore them down and drove them out of his mind for the time; just as men's misfortunes are forgotten in the excitement of new enterprises. This new interest was a valued novelty in whistling, which he had just acquired from a Negro, and he was suffering to practise it undisturbed. It consisted of a peculiar birdlike sound, a sort of liquid warble, produced by touching the tongue to the roof of the mouth at short intervals in the midst of the music. The reader probably remembers how to do it if he has ever been a boy. Diligence and attention soon gave him the knack of it, and he strode down the street with his mouth full of harmony and his soul full of gratitude. He felt much as an astronomer feels who has discovered a new planet. No doubt as far as strong, deep, unalloyed pleasure is concerned, the advantage was with the boy, not the astronomer.

The summer evenings were long. It was not dark yet. Presently Tom checked his whistle. A stranger was before him; a boy a shade larger than himself. A newcomer of any age or either sex

was an impressive curiosity in the poor little village of St Petersburg. This boy was well dressed, too—well dressed on a weekday. This was simply astounding. His cap was a dainty thing, his close-buttoned blue cloth roundabout was new and natty, and so were his pantaloons. He had shoes on, and yet it was only Friday. He even wore a necktie, a bright bit of ribbon. He had a citified air about him that ate into Tom's vitals. The more Tom stared at the splendid marvel, the higher he turned up his nose at his finery, and the shabbier and shabbier his own outfit seemed to him to grow. Neither boy spoke. If one moved the other moved—but only sidewise, in a circle. They kept face to face and eye to eye all the time. Finally, Tom said:

"I can lick you!"

"I'd like to see you try it."

"Well, I can do it."

"No, you can't either."

"Yes, I can."

"No, you can't."

"I can."

"You can't."

"Can."

"Can't."

An uncomfortable pause. Then Tom said:

"What's your name?"

"'Tisn't any of your business, maybe." "Well, I 'low I'll *make* it my business."

"Well, why don't you?"

"If you say much I will."

"Much—much—much! There, now."

"Oh, you think you're mighty smart, *don't* you? I could lick you

with one hand tied behind me, if I wanted to."

"Well, why don't you *do* it? You *say* you can do it."

"Well, I *will*, if you fool with me."

"Oh yes, I've seen whole families in the same fix."

"Smarty! You think you're *some* now, *don't* you?"

"Oh, what a hat!"

"You can lump that hat if you don't like it. I dare you to knock it off; and anybody that'll take a dare will suck eggs."

"You're a liar!"

"You're another."

"You're a fighting liar, and darn't take it up."

"Aw—take a walk!"

"Say—if you give me much more of your sass I'll take and bounce a rock off'n your head."

"Oh, of *course* you will."

"Well, I *will*."

"Well, why don't you *do* it, then? What do you keep *saying* you will, for? Why don't you *do* it? It's because you're afraid."

"I *ain't* afraid."

"You are."

"I ain't."

"You are."

Another pause, and more eyeing and sidling around each other. Presently they were shoulder to shoulder. Tom said:

"Get away from here!"

"Get away yourself!"

"I won't."

"*I* won't, either."

So they stood, each with a foot placed at an angle as a brace, and both shoving with might and main, and glowering at each

other with hate. But neither could get an advantage. After struggling till both were hot and flushed, each relaxed his strain with watchful caution, and Tom said:

"You're a coward and a pup. I'll tell my big brother on you, and he can beat you with his little finger, and I'll make him do it, too."

"What do I care for your big brother? I've got a brother that's bigger than he is; and, what's more, he can throw him over that fence, too." (Both brothers were imaginary.)

"That's a lie."

"*Your* saying so don't make it so."

Tom drew a line in the dust with his big toe, and said:

"I dare you to step over that, and I'll lick you till you can't stand up. Anybody that'll take a dare will steal a sheep."

The new boy stepped over promptly and said:

"Now you said you'd do it, now let's see you do it."

"Don't you crowd me, now. You'd better look out."

"Well, you *said* you'd do it—why don't you do it?"

"By jingoes, for two cents I *will* do it."

The new boy took two broad coppers out of his pocket and held them out with derision.

Tom struck them to the ground.

In an instant both boys were rolling and tumbling in the dirt, gripped together like cats; and for the space of a minute they tugged and tore at each other's hair and clothes, punched and scratched each other's noses, and covered themselves with dust and glory. Presently the confusion took form, and through the fog of battle Tom appeared, seated astride the new boy, and pounding him with his fists.

"Holler 'nuff!" said he.

The boy only struggled to free himself. He was crying, mainly from rage.

"Holler 'nuff!" and the pounding went on.

At last the stranger got out a smothered "'nuff!" and Tom let him up, and said, "Now that'll learn you. Better look out who you're fooling with next time."

The new boy went off brushing the dust from his clothes, sobbing, snuffling, and occasionally looking back and shaking his head, and threatening what he would do to Tom the "next time he caught him out". To which Tom responded with jeers, and started off in high feather; and as soon as his back was turned the new boy snatched up a stone, threw it, and hit him between the shoulders, and then turned tail and ran like an antelope. Tom chased the traitor home, and thus found out where he lived. He then held a position at the gate for some time, daring the enemy to come outside; but the enemy only made faces at him through the window, and declined. At last the enemy's mother appeared, and called Tom a bad, vicious, vulgar child, and ordered him away. So he went away, but he said he "'lowed" to "lag" for that boy.

He got home pretty late that night, and when he climbed cautiously in at the window he found his aunt waiting for him, and when she saw the state his clothes were in, her resolution to turn his Saturday holiday into captivity at hard labour became adamantine in its firmness.

Chapter Two
The Artist at Work

Saturday morning came and all the summer world was bright and fresh. The locust trees were in bloom, and the fragrance of the blossoms filled the air.

Cardiff Hill, beyond the village and above it, was green with vegetation, and it lay just far enough away to seem a Delectable Land, dreamy, reposeful and Inviting.

Tom appeared on the sidewalk with a bucket of whitewash and a long-handled brush. He surveyed the fence, and a deep melancholy settled down upon his spirit. Thirty yards of broad fence nine feet high! It seemed to him that life was hollow, and existence but a burden. Sighing, he dipped his brush and passed it along the topmost plank; repeated the operation, did it again; compared the insignificant whitewashed streak with the far-reaching continent of unwhitewashed fence, and sat down on a tree box, discouraged. Jim came skipping out at the gate with a tin pail, and singing "Buffalo Gals". Bringing water from the town pump had always been hateful work in Tom's eyes before, but now it did not strike him so. He remembered that there was company at the pump. White, mulatto, and Negro boys and girls were always there waiting their turns, resting, trading play-things, quarrelling, fighting, skylarking. And he remembered that although the pump was only a hundred and fifty yards off, Jim never got back with a bucket of water under an hour; and even then somebody generally had to go after him. Tom said:

"Say, Jim, I'll fetch the water if you'll whitewash some."

Jim shook his head, and said:

"Can't, Ma'rs Tom. Ole missus she tole me I got to go an' git dis water an' not stop foolin' 'roun wid anybody. She say she spec' Ma'rs Tom gwyne to ax me to whitewash, an' so she tole me go 'long an' 'tend to my own business—she 'lowed *she*'d 'tend to de whitewashin'."

"Oh, never you mind what she said, Jim. That's the way she always talks. Gimme the bucket—I won't be gone only a minute. *She* won't ever know."

"Oh, I dasn't, Ma'rs Tom. Ole missus she'd take an' tar de head off'n me. 'Deed she would."

"*She*! She never licks anybody—whacks 'em over the head with her thimble, and who cares for that, I'd like to know? She talks awful, but talk don't hurt—anyways, it don't if she don't cry. Jim, I'll give you a marble. I'll give you a white alley!"

Jim began to waver.

"White alley, Jim; and it's a bully tow."

"My! Dat's a mighty gay marvel, I tell you. But, Ma'rs Tom, I's powerful 'fraid ole missus."

But Jim was only human—this attraction was too much for him. He put down his pail, took the white alley. In another minute he was flying down the street with his pail and a tingling rear, Tom was whitewashing with vigour, and Aunt Polly was retiring from the field with a slipper in her hand and triumph in her eye.

But Tom's energy did not last. He began to think of the fun he had planned for this day, and his sorrows multiplied. Soon the free boys would come tripping along on all sorts of delicious expeditions, and they would make a world of fun of him for having to work—the very thought of it burnt him like fire. He

got out his worldly wealth and examined it—bits of toys, marbles, and trash; enough to buy an exchange of work maybe, but not enough to buy so much as half-an-hour of pure freedom. So he returned his straitened means to his pocket, and gave up the idea of trying to buy the boys. At this dark and hopeless moment an inspiration burst upon him. Nothing less than a great, magnificent inspiration. He took up his brush and went tranquilly to work. Ben Rogers hove in sight presently; the very boy of all boys whose ridicule he had been dreading. Ben's gait was the hop, skip and jump—proof enough that his heart was light and his anticipations high. He was eating an apple, and giving a long, melodious whoop at intervals, followed by a deep-toned ding dong dong, dong dong dong, for he was personating a steamboat. As he drew near he slackened speed, took the middle of the street, leaned far over to starboard, and rounded-to ponderously, and with laborious pomp and circumstance, for he was personating the *Big Missouri*, and considered himself to be drawing nine feet of water. He was boat, and captain, and engine bells all combined into one, so he had to imagine himself standing on his own hurricane deck, giving the orders and executing them.

"Stop her, sir! Ling-a-ling-ling." The headway ran almost out, and he drew up slowly toward the sidewalk. "Ship up to back! Ling-a-ling-ling!" His arms straightened and stiffened down his sides. "Set her back on the stabboard! Ling-a-ling-ling! Chow! Ch-chow-wow-chow!" his right hand meantime describing stately circles, for it was representing a forty-foot wheel. "Let her go back on the labboard! Ling-a-ling-ling! Chow-ch-chow-chow!" The left hand began to describe circles.

"Stop the stabboard! Ling-a-ling-ling! Stop the labboard! Come

ahead on the stabboard! Stop her! Let your outside turn over slow! Ling-a-ling-ling! Chow-ow-ow! Get out that head line! Lively, now! Come—out with your spring line—what're you about there? Take a turn round that stump with the bight of it! Stand by that stage now—let her go! Done with the engines, sir! Ling-a-ling-ling!"

"Sht! s'sht! sht!" (Trying the gauge cocks.)

Tom went on whitewashing—paid no attention to the steamer. Ben stared a moment, and then said:

"Hi-yi! You're up a stump, ain't you!"

No answer. Tom surveyed his last touch with the eye of an artist, then he gave his brush another gentle sweep, and surveyed the result as before. Ben ranged up alongside of him. Tom's mouth watered for the apple, but he stuck to his work. Ben said:

"Hello, old chap! You got to work, hey?"

"Why, it's you, Ben! I warn't noticing."

"Say, I'm going in a-swimming, I am. Don't you wish you could? But of course you'd druther work, wouldn't you? 'Course you would!"

Tom contemplated the boy a bit, and said:

"What do you call work?"

"Why, ain't that work?"

Tom resumed his whitewashing, and answered carelessly:

"Well, maybe it is, and maybe it ain't. All I know is, it suits Tom Sawyer."

"Oh, come now, you don't mean to let on that you like it?"

The brush continued to move.

"Like it? Well, I don't see why I oughtn't to like it. Does a boy get a chance to whitewash a fence every day?"

That put the thing in a new light. Ben stopped nibbling his

apple. Tom swept his brush daintily back and forth—stepped back to note the effect—added a touch here and there—criticized the effect again, Ben watching every move and getting more and more interested, more and more absorbed. Presently he said:

"Say, Tom, let me whitewash a little."

Tom considered, was about to consent, but he altered his mind: "No, no. I reckon it wouldn't hardly do, Ben. You see, Aunt Polly's awful particular about this fence—right here on the street, you know—but if it was the back fence I wouldn't mind, and she wouldn't. Yes, she's awful particular about this fence. It's got to be done very careful. I reckon there ain't one boy in a thousand, maybe two thousand, that can do it the way it's got to be done."

"No—is that so? Oh, come now; lemme just try, only just a little. I'd let you, if you was me, Tom."

"Ben, I'd like to, honest injun; but Aunt Polly—well, Jim wanted to do it, but she wouldn't let him. Sid wanted to do it, but she wouldn't let Sid. Now, don't you see how I am fixed? If you was to tackle this fence, and anything was to happen to it—"

"Oh, shucks; I'll be just as careful. Now lemme try. Say—I'll give you the core of my apple."

"Well, here. No, Ben; now don't; I'm afeard—"

"I'll give you all of it!"

Tom gave up the brush with reluctance in his face, but alacrity in his heart. And while the late steamer *Big Missouri* worked and sweated in the sun, the retired artist sat on a barrel in the shade close by, dangled his legs, munched his apple, and planned the slaughter of more innocents. There was no lack of material. Boys happened along every little while; they came to jeer, but remained

to whitewash. By the time Ben was fagged out, Tom had traded the next chance to Billy Fisher for a kite in good repair; and when he played out, Johnny Miller bought in for a dead rat and a string to swing it with; and so on, and so on, hour after hour. And when the middle of the afternoon came, from being a poor poverty-stricken boy in the morning, Tom was literally rolling in wealth. He had, besides the things I have mentioned, twelve marbles, part of a Jew's harp, a piece of blue bottle glass to look through, a spool cannon, a key that wouldn't unlock anything, a fragment of chalk, a glass stopper of a decanter, a tin soldier, a couple of tadpoles, six firecrackers, a kitten with only one eye, a brass doorknob, a dog collar—but no dog —the handle of a knife, four pieces of orange peel, and a dilapidated old window sash. He had had a nice, good, idle time all the while—plenty of company—and the fence had three coats of whitewash on it! If he hadn't run out of whitewash, he would have bankrupted every boy in the village.

Tom said to himself that it was not such a hollow world after all. He had discovered a great law of human action, without knowing it, namely, that in order to make a man or a boy covet a thing, it is only necessary to make the thing difficult to attain. If he had been a great and wise philosopher, like the writer of this book, he would now have comprehended that work consists of whatever a body is obliged to do, and that play consists of whatever a body is not obliged to do. And this would help him to understand why constructing artificial flowers or performing on a treadmill, is work, whilst rolling ninepins or climbing Mont Blanc is only amusement. There are wealthy gentlemen in England who drive four-horse passenger coaches twenty to thirty miles on a daily line, in the summer, because the privilege costs

them considerable money; but if they were offered wages for the service, that would turn it into work, and then they would resign.

Chapter Three

The Artist in Love

Tom presented himself before Aunt Polly, who was sitting by an open window in a pleasant rearward apartment which was bedroom, breakfast room, dining room, and library combined. The balmy summer air, the restful quiet, the odour of the flowers, and the drowsing murmur of the bees had had their effect, and she was nodding over her knitting—for she had no company but the cat, and it was asleep in her lap. Her spectacles were propped up on her grey head for safety. She had thought that of course Tom had deserted long ago, and she wondered to see him place himself in her power again in this intrepid way. He said:

"Mayn't I go and play now, aunt?"

"What, a'ready? How much have you done?"

"It's all done, aunt."

"Tom, don't lie to me. I can't bear it."

"I ain't, aunt. It *is* all done."

Aunt Polly placed small trust in such evidence. She went out to see for herself, and she would have been content to find twenty per cent of Tom's statement true. When she found the entire fence whitewashed, and not only whitewashed but elaborately coated and recoated, and even a streak added to the ground,

her astonishment was almost unspeakable. She said:

"Well, I never! There's no getting around it; you *can* work when you're a mind to, Tom." And then she diluted the compliment by adding, "But it's powerful seldom you're a mind to, I'm bound to say. Well, go 'long and play, but mind you get back some time in a week, or I'll tan you."

She was so overcome by the splendour of his achievement that she took him into the closet and selected a choice apple, and delivered it to him, along with an improving lecture upon the added value and flavour a treat took to itself when it came without sin through virtuous effort. And while she closed with a happy Scriptural flourish, he "hooked" a doughnut.

Then he skipped out, and saw Sid just starting up the outside stairway that led to the back rooms on the second floor. Clods were handy, and the air was full of them in a twinkling. They raged around Sid like a hailstorm; and before Aunt Polly could collect her surprised faculties and rally to the rescue, six or seven clods had taken personal effect, and Tom was over the fence and gone. There was a gate, but as a general thing he was too crowded for time to make use of it. His soul was at peace, now that he had settled with Sid for calling attention to his black thread and getting him into trouble.

Tom skirted the block and came around into a muddy alley that led by the back of his aunt's cow stable. He presently got safely beyond the reach of capture and punishment, and wended towards the public square of the village, where two "military" companies of boys had met for conflict, according to previous appointment. Tom was general of one of these armies, Joe Harper (a bosom friend) general of the other. These two great commanders did not condescend to fight in person—that being

better suited to the smaller fry—but sat together on an eminence and conducted the field operations by orders delivered through aides-de-camp. Tom's army won a great victory, after a long and hard-fought battle. Then the dead were counted, prisoners exchanged, the terms of the next disagreement agreed upon, and the day for the necessary battle appointed; after which the armies fell into line and marched away, and Tom turned homeward alone.

As he was passing by the house where Jeff Thatcher lived, he saw a new girl in the garden—a lovely little blue-eyed creature with yellow hair plaited into two long tails, white summer frock, and embroidered pantalettes. The fresh-crowned hero fell without firing a shot. A certain Amy Lawrence vanished out of his heart and left not even a memory of herself behind. He had thought he loved her to distraction; he had regarded his passion as adoration; and behold it was only a poor little evanescent partiality. He had been months winning her, she had confessed hardly a week ago; he had been the happiest and the proudest boy in the world only seven short days, and here, in one instant of time, she had gone out of his heart like a casual stranger whose visit is done.

He worshipped this new angel with furtive eye, till he saw that she had discovered him; then he pretended he did not know she was present, and began to "show off" in all sorts of absurd boyish ways in order to win her admiration. He kept up this grotesque foolishness for some little time; but by and by, while he was in the midst of some dangerous gymnastic performances, he glanced aside, and saw that the little girl was wending towards the house. Tom came up to the fence, and leaned on it, grieving, and hoping she would stay yet a while longer. She halted

a moment on the steps, and then moved towards the door. Tom heaved a great sigh as she put her foot on the threshold, but his face lit up, right away, for she tossed a pansy over the fence a moment before she disappeared. The boy ran around and stopped within a foot or two of the flower, and then shaded his eyes with his hand and began to look down street as if he had discovered something of interest going on in that direction. Presently he picked up a straw and began trying to balance it on his nose, with his head tilted far back, and as he moved from side to side in his efforts he edged nearer and nearer towards the pansy; finally his bare foot rested upon it, his pliant toes closed upon it, and he hopped away with his treasure and disappeared around the corner. But only for a minute—only while he could button the flower inside his jacket, next his heart, or next his stomach possibly, for he was not much posted in anatomy and not hypercritical anyway.

He returned now and hung about the fence till nightfall, "showing off" as before, but the girl never showed herself again, though Tom comforted himself a little with the hope that she had been near some window meantime, and been aware of his attentions. Finally, he went home reluctantly with his poor head full of visions.

All through supper his spirits were so high that his aunt wondered "what had got into the child". He took a good scolding about clodding Sid, and did not seem to mind it in the least. He tried to steal sugar under his aunt's very nose, and got his knuckles rapped for it. He said:

"Aunt, you don't whack Sid when he takes it."

"Well, Sid don't torment a body the way you do. You'd be always into that sugar if I warn't watching you."

Presently she stepped into the kitchen, and Sid, happy in his immunity, reached for the sugar bowl, a sort of glorying over Tom which was well-nigh unbearable. But Sid's fingers slipped, and the bowl dropped and broke. Tom was in ecstasies—in such ecstasies that he even controlled his tongue and was silent. He said to himself that he would not speak a word, even when his aunt came in, but would sit perfectly still till she asked who did the mischief, and then he would tell, and there would be nothing so good in the world as to see that pet model "catch it". He was so brimful of exultation that he could hardly hold himself when the old lady came back and stood above the wreck discharging lightnings of wrath from over her spectacles. He said to himself, "Now it's coming!" And the next instant he was sprawling on the floor! The potent palm was uplifted to strike again, when Tom cried out:

"Hold on, now, what're you belting *me* for? Sid broke it!"

Aunt Polly paused, perplexed, and Tom looked for healing pity. But when she got her tongue again she only said:

"Umph! Well, you didn't get a lick amiss, I reckon. You'd been into some other owdacious mischief when I wasn't around, like enough."

Then her conscience reproached her, and she yearned to say something kind and loving, but she judged that this would be construed into a confession that she had been in the wrong, and discipline forbade that. So she kept silence, and went about her affairs with a troubled heart. Tom sulked in a corner, and exalted his woes. He knew that in her heart his aunt was on her knees to him, and he was morosely gratified by the consciousness of it. He would hang out no signals, he would take notice of none. He knew that a yearning glance fell upon him, now and

then, through a film of tears, but he refused recognition of it. He pictured himself lying sick unto death and his aunt bending over him, beseeching one little forgiving word, but he would turn his face to the wall, and die with that word unsaid. Ah, how would she feel then? And he pictured himself brought home from the river, dead, with his curls all wet, and his poor hands still for ever, and his sore heart at rest. How she would throw herself upon him, and how her tears would fall like rain, and her lips pray God to give her back her boy, and she would never, never, abuse him any more! But he would lie there cold and white and make no sign—a poor little sufferer whose griefs were at an end. He so worked upon his feelings with the pathos of these dreams that he had to keep swallowing—he was so like to choke; and his eyes swam in a blur of water, which overflowed when he winked, and ran down and trickled from the end of his nose. And such a luxury to him was this petting of his sorrow, that he could not bear to have any worldly cheeriness or any grating delight intrude upon it; it was too sacred for such contact; and so presently, when his cousin Mary danced in, all alive with joy of seeing home again after an age-long visit of one week to the country, he got up and moved in clouds and darkness out at one door as she brought song and sunshine in at the other. He wandered far away from the accustomed haunts of boys, and sought desolate places that were in harmony with his spirits. A log raft in the river invited him, and he seated himself on its outer edge, and contemplated the dreary vastness of the stream, wishing the while that he could only be drowned all at once and unconsciously, without undergoing the uncomfortable routine devised by nature. Then he thought of his flower. He got it out, rumpled and wilted, and it mightily increased his

dismal feeling. He wondered if *she* would pity him if she knew? Would she cry, and wish that she had a right to put her arms around his neck and comfort him? Or would she turn coldly away like all the hollow world? This picture brought such an agony of pleasurable suffering that he worked it over and over again in his mind and set it up in new and varied lights till he wore it threadbare. At last he rose up sighing and departed in the darkness. About half-past nine or ten o'clock he came along the deserted street to where the adored unknown lived; he paused a moment, no sound fell upon his listening ear; a candle was casting a dull glow upon the curtain of a second-storey window. Was the sacred presence there? He climbed the fence, threaded his stealthy way through the plants, till he stood under that window. He looked up at it long, and with emotion; then he laid him down on the ground under it, disposing himself upon his back, with his hands clasped upon his breast, and holding his poor wilted flower. And thus he would die—out in the cold world with no shelter over his homeless head, no friendly hand to wipe the death damps from his brow, no loving face to bend pityingly over him when the great agony came. And thus *she* would see him when she looked out upon the glad morning—and oh, would she drop one tear upon his poor lifeless form; would she heave one little sigh to see a bright young life so rudely blighted, so untimely cut down?

The window went up; a maidservant's discordant voice profaned the holy calm, and a deluge of water drenched the prone martyr's remains!

The strangling hero sprang up with a relieving snort; there was a whiz as of a missile in the air, mingled with the murmur of a curse, a sound as of shivering glass followed, and a small vague

form went over the fence and shot away in the gloom.

Not long after, as Tom, all undressed for bed, was surveying his drenched garments by the light of a tallow dip, Sid woke up; but if he had any dim idea of making "references to allusions", he thought better of it, and held his peace—for there was danger in Tom's eye. Tom turned in without the added vexation of prayers, and Sid made mental note of the omission.

Chapter Four
Sunday School

The sun rose upon a tranquil world, and beamed down upon the peaceful village like a benediction. Breakfast over, Aunt Polly had family worship; it began with a prayer built from the ground up of solid courses of scriptural quotations wedded together with a thin mortar of originality; and from the summit of this she delivered a grim chapter of the Mosaic Law, as from Sinai.

Then Tom girded up his loins, so to speak, and went to work to "get his verses". Sid had learned his lesson days before. Tom bent all his energies to the memorizing of five verses; and he chose part of the Sermon on the Mount, because he could find no verses that were shorter.

At the end of half-an-hour Tom had a vague general idea of his lesson, but no more, for his mind was traversing the whole field of human thought, and his hands were busy with distracting recreations. Mary took his book to hear him recite, and he tried to find his way through the fog.

"Blessed are the—a—a——"

"Poor——"

"Yes—poor; blessed are the poor—a—a——"

"In spirit——"

"In spirit; blessed are the poor in spirit, for they—they——"

"Theirs——"

"For theirs. Blessed are the poor in spirit, for theirs—is the kingdom of heaven. Blessed are they that mourn, for they—they——"

"Sh——"

"For they—a——"

"S-H-A——"

"For they S-H——. Oh, I don't know what it is!"

"Shall!"

"Oh, shall! For they shall—for they shall—a—a—shall mourn—a—a—blessed are they that shall—they that—a—they that shall mourn, for they shall—a—shall what? Why don't you tell me, Mary? What do you want to be so mean for?"

"Oh, Tom, you poor thickheaded thing, I'm not teasing you. I wouldn't do that. You must go and learn it again. Don't you be discouraged, Tom, you'll manage it—and if you do, I'll give you something ever so nice! There, now, that's a good boy."

"All right! What is it, Mary? Tell me what it is."

"Never you mind, Tom. You know if I say it's nice, it's nice."

"You bet you that's so, Mary. All right, I'll tackle it again."

And he did "tackle it again"; and under the double pressure of curiosity and prospective gain, he did it with such spirit that he accomplished a shining success.

Mary gave him a bran-new "Barlow" knife, worth twelve and a half cents; and the convulsion of delight that swept his system shook him to his foundations. True, the knife would not cut any-

thing, but it was a "sure-enough" Barlow, and there was inconceivable grandeur in that—though where the western boys ever got the idea that such a weapon could possibly be counterfeited to its injury, is an imposing mystery, and will always remain so, perhaps. Tom contrived to scarify the cupboard with it and was arranging to begin on the bureau, when he was called off to dress for Sunday school.

Mary gave him a tin basin of water and a piece of soap, and he went outside the door and set the basin on a little bench there; then he dipped the soap in the water and laid it down; turned up his sleeves; poured out the water on the ground gently, and then entered the kitchen, and began to wipe his face diligently on the towel behind the door. But Mary removed the towel and said:

"Now ain't you ashamed, Tom? You mustn't be so bad. Water won't hurt you."

Tom was a trifle disconcerted. The basin was refilled and this time he stood over it a little while, gathering resolution; took in a big breath and began. When he entered the kitchen presently, with both eyes shut, and groping for the towel with his hands, an honourable testimony of suds and water was dripping from his face. But when he emerged from the towel, he was not yet satisfactory; for the clean territory stopped short at his chin and his jaws like a mask; below and beyond this line there was a dark expanse of unirrigated soil that spread downward in front and backward around his neck. Mary took him in hand, and when she was done with him he was a man and a brother, without distinction of colour, and his saturated hair was neatly brushed, and its short curls wrought into a dainty and symmetrical general effect. (He privately smoothed out the curls, with labour

and difficulty, and plastered his hair close down to his head; for he held curls to be effeminate, and his own filled his life with bitterness.) Then Mary got out a suit of his clothing that had been used only on Sundays during two years—they were simply called his "other clothes"—and so by that we know the size of his wardrobe. The girl "put him to rights" after he had dressed himself; she buttoned his neat roundabout up to his chin, turned his vast shirt collar down over his shoulders, brushed him off and crowned him with his speckled straw hat. He now looked exceedingly improved and uncomfortable; and he was fully as uncomfortable as he looked, for there was a restraint about whole clothes and cleanliness that galled him. He hoped that Mary would forget his shoes, but the hope was blighted. She coated them thoroughly with tallow, as was the custom, and brought them out. He lost his temper and said he was always being made to do everything he didn't want to do. But Mary said persuasively:

"Please, Tom—that's a good boy."

So he got into his shoes, snarling. Mary was soon ready, and the three children set out for Sunday school, a place that Tom hated with his whole heart; but Sid and Mary were fond of it.

Sabbath-school hours were from nine to half-past ten; and then church service. Two of the children always remained for the sermon voluntarily, and the other always remained, too—for stronger reasons. The church's high-backed uncushioned pews would seat about three hundred persons; the edifice was but a small, plain affair, with a sort of pine-board tree box on top of it for a steeple. At the door Tom dropped back a step and accosted a Sunday-dressed comrade:

"Say, Bill, got a yaller ticket?"

"Yes."

"What'll you take for her?"

"What'll you give?"

"Piece of lickrish and a fish-hook."

"Less see 'em."

Tom exhibited. They were satisfactory, and the property changed hands. Then Tom traded a couple of white alleys for three red tickets, and some small trifle or other for a couple of blue ones. He waylaid other boys as they came, and went on buying tickets of various colours ten or fifteen minutes longer. He entered the church, now, with a swarm of clean and noisy boys and girls, proceeded to his seat and started a quarrel with the first boy that came handy. The teacher, a grave, elderly man, interfered; then turned his back a moment, and Tom pulled a boy's hair in the next bench, and was absorbed in his book when the boy turned around; stuck a pin in another boy, presently, in order to hear him say "Ouch!" and got a new reprimand from his teacher. Tom's whole class were of a pattern—restless, noisy, and troublesome. When they came to recite their lessons, not one of them knew his verses perfectly, but had to be prompted all along. However, they worried through, and each got his reward in small blue tickets, each with a passage of Scripture on it; each blue ticket was pay for two verses of the recitation. Ten blue tickets equalled a red one, and could be exchanged for it; ten red tickets equalled a yellow one; for ten yellow tickets the Superintendent gave a very plainly bound Bible (worth forty cents in those easy times) to the pupil. How many of my readers would have the industry and the application to memorize two thousand verses, even for a Doré Bible? And yet Mary had acquired two Bibles in this way. It was the patient work of two

years, and a boy of German parentage had won four or five. He once recited three thousand verses without stopping, but the strain upon his mental faculties was too great, and he was little better than an idiot from that day forth—a grievous misfortune for the school, for on great occasions before company, the Superintendent (as Tom expressed it) had always made this boy come out and "spread himself". Only the older pupils managed to keep their tickets and stick to their tedious work long enough to get a Bible, and so the delivery of one of these prizes was a rare and noteworthy circumstance. The successful pupil was so great and conspicuous for that day that on the spot every scholar's breast was fired with a fresh ambition that often lasted a couple of weeks. It is possible that Tom's mental stomach had never really hungered for one of those prizes, but unquestionably his entire being had for many a day longed for the glory and the éclat that came with it.

In due course the Superintendent stood up in front of the pulpit, with a closed hymn book in his hand and his forefinger inserted between its leaves, and commanded attention. When a Sunday-school superintendent makes his customary little speech, a hymn book in the hand is as necessary as is the inevitable sheet of music in the hand of a singer who stands forward on the platform and sings a solo at a concert—though why is a mystery; for neither the hymn book nor the sheet of music is even referred to by the sufferer. This superintendent was a slim creature of thirty-five, with a sandy goatee, and short sandy hair; he wore a stiff standing collar whose upper edge almost reached his ears, and whose sharp points curved forward abreast the corners of his mouth—a fence that compelled a straight lookout ahead, and a turning of the whole body when a side view

was required. His chin was propped on a spreading cravat, which was as broad and as long as a banknote, and had fringed ends his boot toes were turned sharply up, in the fashion of the day like sleigh-runners—an effect patiently and laboriously produced by the young men by sitting with their toes pressed against a wall for hours together. Mr Walters was very earnest of mind and very sincere and honest at heart, and he held sacred things and places in such reverence, and so separated them from worldly matters, that unconsciously to himself his Sunday-school voice had acquired a peculiar intonation which was wholly absent on weekdays. He began after this fashion:

"Now, children, I want you all to sit up just as straight and pretty as you can, and give me all your attention for a minute or two. There, that is it. That is the way good little boys and girl should do. I see one little girl who is looking out of the window—I am afraid she thinks I am out there somewhere—perhaps up in one of the trees making a speech to the little birds. [Applausive titter.] I want to tell you how good it makes me feel to see so many bright, clean little faces assembled in a place like this, learning to do right and be good."

And so forth, and so on. It is not necessary to set down the rest of the oration. It was of a pattern which does not vary, and so it is familiar to us all.

The latter third of the speech was marred by the resumption of fights and other recreations among certain of the bad boys and by fidgetings and whisperings that extended far and wide washing even to the bases of isolated and incorruptible rock like Sid and Mary. But now every sound ceased suddenly with the subsidence of Mr Walters' voice, and the conclusion of the speech was received with a burst of silent gratitude.

A good part of the whispering had been occasioned by an even
which was more or less rare—the entrance of visitors; Lawyer
Thatcher, accompanied by a very feeble and aged man, a fine
portly, middle-aged gentleman with iron-grey hair, and a very
dignified lady who was doubtless the latter's wife. The lady was
leading a child. Tom had been restless and full of chafings and
repinings, conscience-smitten, too—he could not meet Amy
Lawrence's eye, he could not meet her loving gaze. But when he
saw this small newcomer his soul was all ablaze with bliss in a
moment. The next moment he was "showing off" with all hi
might—cuffing boys, pulling hair, making faces, in a word
using every art that seemed likely to him to fascinate a girl, and
win her applause. His exultation had but one alloy—the memory
of his humiliation in this angel's garden; and that record in sand
was fast washing out under the waves of happiness that were
sweeping over it now. The visitors were given the highest seat of
honour, and as soon as Mr Walters' speech was finished, he
introduced them to the school. The middle-aged man turned
out to be a prodigious personage; no less an one than the county
judge—altogether the most august creation these children had
ever looked upon; and they wondered what kind of material he
was made of; and they half wanted to hear him roar, and were
half afraid he might, too. He was from Constantinople, twelve
miles away—so he had most certainly travelled and seen the
world—these very eyes had looked upon the County Court
House, which was said to have a tin roof. The awe which these
reflections inspired was attested by the impressive silence and
the ranks of staring eyes. This was the great Judge Thatcher
brother of their own lawyer. Jeff Thatcher immediately went
forward to be familiar with the great man and be envied by the

school. It would have been music to his soul to hear the whis
perings.

"Look at him, Jim! He's a-going up there. Say look! He's a
going to shake hands with him; he is a shaking hands with him
By jinks, don't you wish you was Jeff?"

Mr Walters fell to "showing off" with all sorts of officia
bustlings and activities, giving orders, delivering judgments, dis
charging directions here, there, and everywhere that he coul
find a target. The librarian "showed off", running hither an
thither with his arms full of books and making a deal of th
splutter and fuss that insect authority delights in. The youn
lady teachers "showed off"—bending sweetly over pupils tha
were lately being boxed, lifting pretty warning fingers at ba
little boys and patting good ones lovingly. The young gentle
man teachers "showed off" with small scoldings and other littl
displays of authority and fine attention to discipline; and mos
of the teachers, of both sexes, found business up at the librar
by the pulpit; and it was business that frequently had to be don
over again two or three times (with much seeming vexation
The little girls "showed off" in various ways, and the little boy
"showed off" with such diligence that the air was thick wit
paper wads and the murmur of scufflings. And above it all th
great man sat and beamed a majestic judicial smile upon all th
house, and warmed himself in the sun of his own grandeur, fo
he was "showing off" too. There was only one thing wanting t
make Mr Walters' ecstasy complete, and that was a chance t
deliver a Bible prize and exhibit a prodigy. Several pupils had
few yellow tickets, but none had enough—he had been aroun
among the star pupils inquiring. He would have given world
now, to have that German lad back again with a sound mind.

And now at this moment, when hope was dead, Tom Sawye
came forward with nine yellow tickets, nine red tickets, and te
blue ones, and demanded a Bible! This was a thunderbolt ou
of a clear sky. Walters was not expecting an application from
this source for the next ten years. But there was no getting aroun
it—here were the certified checks, and they were good for thei
face. Tom was therefore elevated to a place with the Judge an
the other elect, and the great news was announced from head
quarters. It was the most stunning surprise of the decade; an
so profound was the sensation that it lifted the new hero up t
the judicial one's altitude, and the school had two marvels t
gaze upon in place of one. The boys were all eaten up with env
but those that suffered the bitterest pangs were those who per
ceived too late that they themselves had contributed to this hate
splendour by trading tickets to Tom for the wealth he ha
amassed in selling whitewashing privileges. These despised them
selves as being the dupes of a wily fraud, a guileful snake in th
grass.

The prize was delivered to Tom with as much effusion as th
Superintendent could pump up under the circumstances; but i
lacked somewhat of the true gush, for the poor fellow's instinc
taught him that there was a mystery here that could not well
bear the light, perhaps; it was simply preposterous that this bo
had warehoused two thousand sheaves of Scriptural wisdom o
his premises—a dozen would strain his capacity, without a doub
Amy Lawrence was proud and glad, and she tried to make Tor
see it in her face, but he wouldn't look. She wondered; then sh
was just a grain troubled; next a dim suspicion came and went—
came again; she watched; a furtive glance told her worlds—an
then her heart broke, and she was jealous, and angry, and th

tears came and she hated everybody; Tom most of all, she thought.

Tom was introduced to the Judge; but his tongue was tied, his breath would hardly come, his heart quaked—partly because of the awful greatness of the man, but mainly because he was her parent. He would have liked to fall down and worship him, if it were in the dark. The Judge put his hand on Tom's head and called him a fine little man, and asked him what his name was. The boy stammered, gasped, and got it out.

"Tom."

"Oh no, not Tom—it is———"

"Thomas."

"Ah, that's it. I thought there was more to it. That's very well. But you've another one, I think, and you'll tell me it, won't you?"

"Tell the gentleman your other name, Thomas," said Walters, "and say 'sir'. You mustn't forget your manners."

"Thomas Sawyer—Sir."

"That's it! That's a good boy. Fine boy. Fine, manly little fellow. Two thousand verses is a great many—very, very great many. And you never can be sorry for the trouble you took to learn them; for knowledge is worth more than anything there is in the world; it's what makes great men and good men; you'll be a great man and a good man yourself some day, Thomas, and then you'll look back and say: It's all owing to the precious Sunday-school privileges of my boyhood; it's all owing to my dear teachers that taught me to learn; it's all owing to the good Superintendent, who encouraged me and watched over me, and gave me a beautiful Bible, a splendid, elegant Bible, to keep and have it all for my own, always; it's all owing to right bringing up! That is what you will say, Thomas; and you wouldn't take any

money for those two thousand verses, then—no, indeed you wouldn't. And now you wouldn't mind telling me and this lady some of the things you've learned—no, I know you wouldn't—for we are proud of little boys that learn. Now no doubt you know the names of all the twelve disciples. Won't you tell us the names of the first two that were appointed?"

Tom was tugging at a button and looking sheepish. He blushed, now, and his eyes fell. Mr Walters' heart sank within him. He said to himself, It is not possible that the boy can answer the simplest question—why *did* the Judge ask him? Yet he felt obliged to speak up and say:

"Answer the gentleman, Thomas—don't be afraid."

Tom still hung fire.

"Now I know you'll tell *me*," said the lady. "The names of the first two disciples were——"

"DAVID AND GOLIATH!"

Let us draw the curtain of charity over the rest of the scene.

Chapter Five

A Day at Prayers

About half-past ten the cracked bell of the small church began to ring, and presently the people began to gather for the morning sermon. The Sunday-school children distributed themselves about the house, and occupied pews with their parents, so as to be under supervision. Aunt Polly came, and Tom and Sid and Mary sat with her, Tom being placed next the aisle in order that he might be as far away from the open window and the

seductive outside summer scenes as possible. The crowd filed up the aisles; the aged and needy postmaster, who had seen better days; the mayor and his wife—for they had a mayor there, among other unnecessaries; the justice of the peace; the widow Douglas, fair, smart, and forty, a generous, good-hearted soul and well-to-do, her hill mansion the only palace in the town, and the most hospitable and much the most lavish in the matter of festivities that St Petersburg could boast; the bent and venerable mayor and Mrs Ward; Lawyer Riverson, the new notable from a distance; next the belle of the village, followed by a troop of lawn-clad and ribbon-decked young heartbreakers; then all the young clerks in town in a body—for they had stood in the vestibule sucking their cane heads, a circling wall of oiled and simpering admirers, till the last girl had run their gauntlet; and last of all came the model boy, Willie Mufferson, taking as heedful care of his mother as if she were cut glass. He always brought his mother to church, and was the pride of all the matrons. The boys all hated him, he was so good; and besides, he had been "thrown up to them" so much. His white handkerchief was hanging out of his pocket behind, as usual on Sundays—accidentally. Tom had no handkerchief and he looked upon boys who had, as snobs. The congregation being fully assembled now, the bell rang once more, to warn laggards and stragglers, and then a solemn hush fell upon the church which was only broken by the tittering and whispering of the choir in the gallery. The choir always tittered and whispered all through service. There was once a church choir that was not ill-bred, but I have forgotten where it was, now. It was a great many years ago, and I can scarcely remember anything about it, but I think it was in some foreign country.

The minister gave out the hymn, and read it through with a relish, in a peculiar style which was much admired in that part of the country. His voice began on a medium key, and climbed steadily up till it reached a certain point, where it bore with strong emphasis upon the topmost word, and then plunged down as if from a springboard.

He was regarded as a wonderful reader. At church "sociables" he was always called upon to read poetry; and when he was through, the ladies would lift up their hands and let them fall helplessly in their laps, and "wall" their eyes, and shake their heads, as much as to say, "Words cannot express it; it is too beautiful, too beautiful for this mortal earth."

After the hymn had been sung, the Rev. Mr Sprague turned himself into a bulletin board and read off "notices" of meetings and societies and things till it seemed that the list would stretch out to the crack of doom—a queer custom which is still kept up in America, even in cities, away here in this age of abundant newspapers. Often the less there is to justify a traditional custom, the harder it is to get rid of it.

And now, the minister prayed. A good, generous prayer it was, and went into details; it pleaded for the Church, and the little children of the Church; for the other churches of the village; for the village itself; for the country; for the State; for the State officers; for the United States; for the churches of the United States; for Congress; for the President; for the officers of the Government; for poor sailors tossed by stormy seas; for the oppressed millions groaning under the heel of European monarchies and Oriental despotisms; for such as have the light and the good tidings, and yet have not eyes to see nor ears to hear withal; for the heathen in the far islands of the sea; and closed with a sup-

plication that the words he was about to speak might find grace and favour, and be as seed sown in fertile ground, yielding in time a grateful harvest of good. Amen.

There was a rustling of dresses, and the standing congregation sat down. The boy whose history this book relates did not enjoy the prayer, he only endured it—if he even did that much. He was restive all through it; he kept tally of the details of the prayer, unconsciously—for he was not listening, but he knew the ground of old and the clergyman's regular route over it—and when a little trifle of new matter was introduced, his ear detected it and his whole nature resented it; he considered additions unfair, and scoundrelly. In the midst of the prayer a fly had lit on the back of the pew in front of him, and tortured his spirit by calmly rubbing its hands together; embracing its head with its arms and polishing it so vigorously that it seemed to almost part company with the body, and the slender thread of a neck was exposed to view; scraping its wings with its hind legs and smoothing them to its body as if they had been coat tails; going through its whole toilet as tranquilly as if it knew it was perfectly safe. As indeed it was; for as sorely as Tom's hands itched to grab for it they did not dare—he believed his soul would be instantly destroyed if he did such a thing while the prayer was going on. But with the closing sentence his hand began to curve and steal forward, and the instant the "Amen" was out, the fly was a prisoner of war. His aunt detected the act, and made him let it go.

The minister gave out his text and droned along monotonously through an argument that was so prosy that many a head by and by began to nod—and yet it was an argument that dealt in limitless fire and brimstone, and thinned the predestined elect down to a company so small as to be hardly worth the saving.

Tom counted the pages of the sermon; after church he always knew how many pages there had been, but he seldom knew anything else about the discourse. However, this time he was really interested for a little while. The minister made a grand and moving picture of the assembling together of the world's hosts at the millennium when the lion and the lamb should lie down together and a little child should lead them. But the pathos, the lesson, the moral of the great spectacle were lost upon the boy; he only thought of the conspicuousness of the principal character before the onlooking nations; his face lit up with the thought, and he said to himself that he wished he could be that child, if it was a tame lion.

Now he lapsed into suffering again as the dry argument was resumed. Presently he reminded himself of a treasure he had, and got it out. It was a large black beetle with formidable jaws— a "pinch-bug", he called it. It was in a percussion-cap box. The first thing the beetle did was to take him by the finger. A natural fillip followed, the beetle went floundering into the aisle, and lit on its back, and the hurt finger went into the boy's mouth. The beetle lay there working its helpless legs, unable to turn over. Tom eyed it, and longed for it, but it was safe out of his reach. Other people, uninterested in the sermon, found relief in the beetle, and they eyed it too.

Presently a vagrant poodle dog came idling along, sad at heart, lazy with the summer softness and the quiet, weary of captivity, sighing for change. He spied the beetle; the drooping tail lifted and wagged. He surveyed the prize; walked around it; smelt of it from a safe distance; walked around it again; grew bolder, and took a closer smell; then lifted his lip, and made a gingerly snatch at it, just missing it; made another, and another; began to enjoy

the diversion; subsided to his stomach with the beetle between his paws, and continued his experiments; grew weary at last, and then indifferent and absent-minded. His head nodded, and little by little his chin descended and touched the enemy, who seized it. There was a sharp yelp, a flirt of the poodle's head, and the beetle fell a couple of yards away and lit on its back once more. The neighbouring spectators shook with a gentle inward joy, several faces went behind fans and handkerchiefs, and Tom was entirely happy. The dog looked foolish, and probably felt so; but there was resentment in his heart, too, and a craving for revenge. So he went to the beetle and began a wary attack on it again; jumping at it from every point of a circle, lighting with his forepaws within an inch of the creature, making even closer snatches at it with his teeth, and jerking his head till his ears flapped again. But he grew tired once more, after a while; tried to amuse himself with a fly, but found no relief; followed an ant around, with his nose close to the floor, and quickly wearied of that; yawned, sighed, forgot the beetle entirely, and sat down on it. Then there was a wild yelp of agony, and the poodle went sailing up the aisle; the yelps continued, and so did the dog; he crossed the house in front of the altar, he flew down the other aisle; he crossed before the doors; he clamoured up the home stretch; his anguish grew with his progress, till presently he was but a woolly comet moving in its orbit with the gleam and the speed of light. At last the frantic sufferer sheered from its course and sprang into its master's lap; he flung it out of the window, and the voice of distress quickly thinned away and died in the distance.

By this time the whole church was red-faced and suffocating with suppressed laughter, and the sermon had come to a dead

standstill. The discourse was resumed presently, but it went lame and halting, all possibility of impressiveness being at an end; for even the gravest sentiments were constantly being received with a smothered burst of unholy mirth, under cover of some remote pew back, as if the poor parson had said a rarely facetious thing. It was a genuine relief to the whole congregation when the ordeal was over and the benediction pronounced.

Tom Sawyer went home quite cheerful, thinking to himself that there was some satisfaction about divine service when there was a bit of variety in it. He had but one marring thought; he was willing that the dog should play with his pinch-bug, but he did not think it was upright in him to carry it off.

Chapter Six
Tom Sits With the Girls

Monday morning found Tom Sawyer miserable.

Monday morning always found him so, because it began another slow week's suffering in school.

His heart was heavy as he made his way along the village street, but his face brightened when he saw Huckleberry Finn coming towards him. Huckleberry, who was an orphan and who looked after himself, was hated and dreaded by all the mothers of the town of St. Petersburg because he was idle, and lawless, and vulgar, and bad—and because all their children admired him so, and delighted in his forbidden society and wished they dared to be like him. Tom was under strict orders not to play with him, so he played with him every time he got a chance.

Huckleberry was always dressed in rags, and came and went at his own free will. He slept on doorsteps in fine weather; he did not have to go to school or church, or call anyone master, or obey anybody; he could go fishing or swimming when and where he chose, and stay as long as it suited him; he could sit up as late as he pleased; he never had to wash, nor put on clean clothes; he could swear wonderfully. In a word, everything that goes to make life precious, this boy had.

"Hello, Huckleberry," said Tom. "What's that you've got?"

"Dead cat."

"Let me see him, Huck. My, he's pretty stiff. What d'you want it for?"

"Cure warts with."

"No? Is that so? How d'you cure them with dead cats?"

"Why, you take your cat and go and get in the graveyard, about midnight, where somebody that was wicked has been buried; and when it's midnight a devil will come, or perhaps two or three; and when they're taking that fellow away, you throw your cat after them and say, 'Devil follow body, cat follow devil, warts follow cat, *I'm* done with you!' That'll cure any wart."

"It sounds all right. When are you going to try the cat?"

"Tonight. I reckon they'll come after old Horse Williams tonight."

"But they buried him on Saturday, Huck. Didn't they get him Saturday night?"

"Why, how you talk! How could their charms work till midnight? And then it was Sunday. Devils don't move around on a Sunday."

"I never thought of that. That's so. Let me go with you?"

"Of course—if you're not afraid."

"Afraid! Not likely! Will you meow outside my window?"

"Yes, and you meow back if you get a chance. Last time you kept me meowing around till old Hays started throwing rocks at me, and shouted, 'Curse that cat!' So I threw a brick through his window—but don't you tell."

"I won't tell. I'll see you later Huck. I'm late for school."

When Tom reached the little school-house, he walked in with the air of one who had come with all honest speed. The master, seated upon his high chair, called to him, angrily:

"Thomas Sawyer! Why are you late again, as usual?"

Tom was about to take refuge in a lie, when he saw two long tails of yellow hair hanging down a back that he recognized by the electric sympathy of love; and by that form was *the only vacant place* on the girls' side of the schoolhouse. He instantly said:

"I STOPPED TO TALK WITH HUCKLEBERRY FINN!"

The master stared; the pupils stared; everybody wondered if this daring boy had lost his mind. The master said:

"You—you did what?"

"Stopped to talk with Huckleberry Finn."

There was no mistaking the words.

"Thomas Sawyer, this is the most astonishing confession to which I have ever listened. You m-ust be punished. Take off your coat."

The master's arm performed until his stick broke in two. Then the order followed:

"Now, sir, go and sit with the *girls!* And let this be a warning to you."

Every eye watched Tom sit down upon the end of the bench, next to the girl with yellow hair and blue eyes. He hung his head as if he was ashamed, but when all attention ceased from him,

he began to steal glances at the girl. She gave him the back of her head for the space of a minute. When she cautiously faced round again, an apple lay before her. She pushed it away; Tom gently put it back; she pushed it away again, but with less determination. Tom patiently returned it to its place; then she let it remain. Tom wrote on his slate: "Please take it—I've got more." The girl glanced at the words, but made no sign.

Now the boy began to draw something on the slate, hiding his work with his left hand. For a time the girl refused to notice, but at last her curiosity got the better of her, and she made an attempt to see. Tom kept his work covered. At last she gave in, and hesitatingly whispered:

"Let me see it."

Tom uncovered a drawing of a house, with smoke pouring out of the chimney. The girl studied it with interest, then whispered:

"It's nice—make a man.

The artist erected in the front yard a man who could have stepped over the house, but the girl was not critical.

"It's ever so nice," she said. "I wish I could draw."

"It's easy," whispered Tom. "I'll teach you."

"Oh, will you? When?"

"At noon. Do you go home to dinner?"

"I'll stay if you will."

"Good—what's your name?"

"Becky Thatcher. And yours is Thomas Sawyer."

"You call me Tom—will you?"

"Yes." Now Tom began to scrawl something on the slate, hiding the words from the girl. But she was not backward this time. She begged to see. Tom said:

"Oh, it's not anything."

"Yes, it is."

"No, it's not; you don't want to see."

"Yes, I do, indeed I do. Please let me."

"You won't tell anybody at all? Ever as long as you live?"

"No, I won't ever tell anybody. Now let me."

"Oh, you don't want to see!"

"Now that you treat me so I *will* see, Tom "—and she put her small hand on his and a little struggle followed, Tom pretending to resist in earnest, but letting his hand slip by degrees till these words were revealed: "I love you."

"Oh, you bad thing!" And she hit his hand, but reddened and looked pleased all the same.

Just at this point the boy felt a strong grip close on his ear. He was lifted to his feet then borne across the room and deposited in his own seat, to the sound of laughter from the whole school. The master stood over him during a few awful moments. At last moved away to his throne without saying a word. But although Tom's ear pained him, his heart was singing within him.

When school broke up at noon, Tom flew to Becky Thatcher, and whispered in her ear:

"Pretend you're going home. When you get to the corner, give the rest of them the slip, and turn down through the lane and come back. I'll be waiting for you."

In a little while the two met at the bottom of the lane, and when they reached the school they had it to themselves. They sat together with a slate before them, and Tom gave Becky the pencil. He held her hand in his, guiding it, and so drew another surprising house. When the two lost interest in art, they fell to talking. Tom was swimming in happiness. He said:

"Becky, were you ever engaged?"

"What's that?"

"Why, engaged to be married."

"No."

"Would you like to?"

"I reckon so. I don't know. What is it like?"

"Well, you just tell a boy you won't ever have anybody but him, ever, ever, *ever*, and then you kiss, and that's all. Anybody can do it."

"Kiss? What do you kiss for?"

"Why that—you know . . . is to—well, they *always* do that."

"Everybody?"

"Yes, everybody that's in love with each other. Do you remember what I wrote on the slate?"

"Ye-es."

"What was it?"

"I shan't tell you."

"Shall I tell *you?* I'll whisper it—I'll whisper it ever so easy."

Becky hesitating, Tom took silence for consent. He passed his arm about her waist and whispered the words ever so softly, with his mouth close to her ear. And then he added:

"Now you whisper it to me—just the same."

She resisted for a while, and then said:

"Turn your face away, so you can't see, and then I will."

He turned his face away. She bent timidly around till her breath stirred his curls, and whispered, "I . . . love . . . you!"

Then she sprang away and ran around and around the desks with Tom after her. She took refuge in a corner at last, with her hands over her face.

"Now, Becky, it's all over—all over but the kiss. Don't be afraid of that—please, Becky."

He pulled at her hands. By-and-by she gave up and let her hands drop; her face, all glowing with the struggle, came up and Tom kissed the red lips, and said:

"Now you're not ever to marry anybody but me, never never and for ever. Will you?"

"No, I'll never love anybody but you, Tom, and I'll never marry anybody but you, and you're not to marry anybody but me, either."

"Certainly. Of course. And always, when there isn't anybody looking, you're to walk to school with me—and you choose me and I choose you at parties, because that's the way you do when you're engaged."

"It's so nice. I never heard of it before."

"Oh, it's ever such fun! Why me and Amy Lawrence—

The big eyes told Tom his mistake, and he stopped, confused.

"Oh, Tom! I'm not the first you've been engaged to!"

The child began to cry. Tom said:

"Oh, don't cry, Becky. I don't care for her any more."

"Yes, you do, Tom—you know you do."

Tom tried to put his arm about her neck, but she pushed him away and turned her face to the wall, and went on crying. Tom tried again, but was pushed away again. He walked away and went outside. He stood about, hoping she would come to find him. But she did not. Then he began to feel badly and fear that he was in the wrong. He went back inside.

She was still standing there in the corner, crying with her face to the wall. Tom went to her and stood a moment, not knowing exactly what to say. Then he said, hesitatingly:

"Becky, I—I don't care for anybody but you."

No reply.

"Becky," in a begging voice.

Only the sound of crying.

Tom got out his chiefest jewel, a brass doorknob, and passed i
around her so that she could see it, and said:

"Please, Becky, won't you take it?"

She struck it to the floor. Then Tom marched out of the build-
ing, and left Becky to her tears. At last she began to suspect. She
ran to the door; he was not in sight; she flew around to the play
yard; he was not there. Then she called:

"Tom! Come back, Tom!"

She listened, but there was no answer. She had no compan
ions but silence and loneliness . . .

Tom had gone over the hills and far away, to return to schoo
no more that day.

Chapter Seven

The Graveyard at Midnight

At half-past nine that night, Tom and Sid were sent to bed a
usual. They said their prayers, and Sid was soon asleep. Tom
lay awake and waited in restless impatience. When it seemed to
him that it must be nearly daylight, he heard the clock strike
ten! At last he was satisfied that time had stopped altogether; he
began to doze in spite of himself; the clock struck eleven, but he
did not hear it. And then there came, all mixed up with his
dreams, a loud meowing. The raising of a neighbouring win
dow disturbed him. A cry of "Clear off, you devil!" and the crash
of an empty bottle against the back of his aunt's wood-shec

brought him wide awake; and a single minute later he wa
dressed and out of the window and creeping on hands and knee
along the roof of the shed. He meowed with caution once o
twice as he went; then jumped down to the ground. Huckleberr
Finn was there, with his dead cat. The boys moved off and van
ished in the darkness. At the end of half an hour they were walk
ing through the tall grass of the graveyard.

A faint wind moaned through the trees, and Tom feared
might be the spirits of the dead complaining at being disturbec
The boys talked little, and only under their breath, for the tim
and the place and the silence weighed heavily upon them. The
found the sharp new heap they were searching for, and hid them
selves within the protection of three great elms that grew in
bunch close to the grave.

The sad call of a distant owl was all the sound that trouble
the dead stillness. Presently Tom seized his friend's arm an
said:

"Sh!"

"What is it, Tom?" And the two clung together with beatin
hearts.

"Sh! There it is again! Didn't you hear it?"

"I—"

"There! Now you hear it!"

"Lordy, Tom, they're coming! They're coming, sure. What'
we do?"

"I don't know. Think they'll see us?"

"Oh, Tom, they can see in the dark same as cats. I wish I hadn
come."

"Oh, don't be afraid. If we keep perfectly still, perhaps the
won't notice us at all."

"I'll try to, Tom, but I'm all of a shiver." "Listen!"

The boys bent their heads together and hardly breathed. A faint sound of voices floated up from the far end of the grave-yard.

"Look! See there!" whispered Tom. "What is it?"

Some vague figures approached through the darkness, swinging an old-fashioned tin lantern that spotted the ground with little circles of light.

Huck whispered, with a shiver: It's the devils, sure enough. Three of them! Lordy, Tom, we're dead men! Can you pray?"

"I'll try, but don't you be afraid. They're not going to—"

"Sh!"

"What is it, Huck?"

"They're *humans!* One of them is, anyway. One of them's old Muff Potter's voice."

"So it is! And I know another of those voices. It's Injun Joe."

"You're right—that murdering half-breed! I'd rather they were devils, Tom. What can they be up to?"

The whispers died away now, for the three men had reached the grave, and stood within a few feet of the boys' hiding-place.

"Here it is," said the third voice; and the owner of it held the lantern up and revealed the face of young Dr. Robinson.

Potter and Injun Joe were carrying a hand-barrow with a rope and a couple of spades on it. They put down their load and began to open the grave. The doctor put the lantern at the head of the grave, and came and sat down with his back against one of the elm-trees. He was so close the boys could have touched him.

"Hurry, men!" he said in a low voice. "The moon might come out at any moment."

For some time, there was no noise but the sound of the spades meeting the earth, and then a blade struck upon the coffin with a dull, woody noise. Within another minute or two the men had lifted it out on the ground. They forced open the lid with their spades, got out the body and laid it on the barrow. A blanket was thrown over it, and it was bound to its place with the rope. Potter took out a large knife and cut off the loose end of rope, then said:

"Now the thing's ready, doctor, and you'll just hand over another five dollars, or here it stays."

"That's the talk!" said Injun Joe.

"Look here, what does this mean?" asked the doctor. "You required your pay in advance and I've paid you."

"Yes, and you've done more than that," said Injun Joe, approaching the doctor, who was now standing. "Five years ago you drove me away from your father's kitchen one night when I came to ask for something to eat. When I swore I'd get even with you, your father had me thrown into jail as a vagrant. Did you think I'd forget? I've got you where I want you, so you had better settle with me, now, you know."

He was threatening the doctor with his fist in his face by this time. The doctor struck out suddenly and stretched the wretch flat out upon the ground. Potter dropped his knife and cried:

"Here, now, don't you strike my partner!"

The next moment he and the doctor were struggling together, and tearing the ground with their heels. Injun Joe sprang to his feet, his eyes flaming with hatred, snatched up Potter's knife and crept, like a cat, around the two fighters, waiting his opportunity. All at once the doctor tore himself free, seized the heavy headboard of Williams's grave and with it knocked Potter to the

earth, unconscious. In the same instant Injun Joe saw his chance, and drove the knife hard into the young man's chest. The doctor fell partly upon Potter, flooding him with his blood, and in the same moment the clouds hid the dreadful spectacle, and the two frightened boys went speeding away in the dark.

When the moon appeared again, Injun Joe was standing over the two still forms, looking down at them. The doctor gave one last choking cry, and was still.

"That's settled *you*, curse you!" the half-breed said between his teeth.

Then he robbed the body. After which he put the knife in Potter's open right hand, and sat down on the coffin. Three—four—five minutes passed, and then Potter made a little sound and began to move. His hand closed upon the knife, he raised it, glanced at it, and let it fall. A violent shiver ran through him. He sat up, pushing the body from him, stared at it and then around him in a confused way. His eyes met Joe's.

"What—what did you do it for?" he said.

"*I!* I never did it!"

Potter grew white and shook even more.

"I'd been drinking, Joe," he said, "and I'd no business to, to-night. I'm all mixed up.

Tell me, Joe—*hones*, now—did I do it? I never meant to. Tell me how it was, Joe."

"Why, you tow were struggling, and he fetched you one with the headboard, and you fell flat; and then up you came again, and snatched the knife and stuck it into him just as he hit you with the board again, and here you've lain like a dead one till now."

"I didn't know what I was doing," groaned Potter. "I never

used a weapon in my life before, Joe. Joe, don't tell! Say you won't tell, Joe—"

The poor creature dropped on his knees before the brute of a murderer, hands joined in a begging attitude, the tears running down his cheeks.

"I won't tell," said Injun Joe. "But come now, that's enough of that. We'd best be off. You go that way, and I'll go this. Move, now, and don't leave any tracks behind you."

Two or three minutes later the murdered man, the blanketed body, the lidless coffin, and the open grave, were being inspected by nothing but the moon. The stillness was complete again.

Chapter Eight
The Noble Boy

The two boys flew on and on towards the village, filled with fright and horror. They glanced backward over their shoulders from time to time, as if they feared they might be followed. Every tree and bush in their path seemed a man and an enemy, and made them catch their breath and run the faster.

At long last they came to a stop in the shadows of a fence, and sank to the ground. By-and-by their breathing became normal, and Tom whispered:

"Huckleberry, what do you reckon will come of this?"

"If Dr. Robinson dies, I reckon hanging will come of it."

Tom thought for a moment, then said:

"Who'll tell? We?"

"What are you talking about? Suppose something happened

and Injun Joe didn't hang, why he'd kill us some time or other, just as sure as we're lying here."

"That's just what I was thinking, Huck."

"If anybody tells, let Muff Potter do it."

"He can't, Huck—he doesn't know about it. How can he tell? He'd just got that hit on the head when Injun Joe knifed the doctor."

"Lordy, that's right, Tom."

There was a thoughtful silence, before Tom said:

"Huck, are you sure you can keep quiet?"

"Tom, we've got to. You know that. That Injun devil would murder us if they didn't hang him. Now look here, Tom, let's swear to one another not to breathe a word."

"I'm agreed, Huck. It's the best thing. Let's do it now."

And there and then the two swore a solemn oath to say nothing concerning the evil deed they had witnessed that night. Then they separated, with much food for thought.

When Tom crept in at his bedroom window, the night was almost spent. He woke late, feeling sore and tired and miserable. He walked, sad and alone, to school, and took a thrashing for his absence of the day before; then took himself to his seat, rested his elbows on his desk and his chin in his hands, and stared at the wall with the fixed stare of suffering that has reached the limit and can no further go. His elbow was pressing against some hard substance. After a long time he slowly and sadly changed his position, and took up this object with a sigh. It was in a paper. He unrolled it. It was his brass doorknob! His heart broke.

Close upon the hour of noon the whole village was shocked by the dreadful news of the young doctor's murder. The tale flew

from man to man, from group to group, from house to house. Of course, the schoolmaster gave a holiday for that afternoon; the town would have thought strangely of him if he had not. A blood-stained knife had been found close to the murdered man, and it had been recognized by somebody as belonging to Muff Potter—so the story ran. And it was said that a man had come upon Potter washing himself in the river about one or two o'clock in the morning, and that Potter had at once crept off—suspicious circumstances, especially the washing, which was not a habit with Potter. The town was being searched for this "murderer", and the Sheriff was confident that he would be captured before night.

All the town was moving towards the graveyard. Tom's heartbreak vanished, and he joined the procession, not because he would not a thousand times rather go anywhere else, but because some terrible force drew him along. As he made his way through the crowd, somebody touched his arm. He turned, and his eyes met Huckleberry's. Huckleberry nodded his head and Tom, following his glance, shivered from head to heel; for his eye fell upon the cruel face of Injun Joe. At this moment the crowd began to part, and voices shouted, "It's him! it's him!"

The Sheriff came through, leading Potter by the arm. The poor fellow's face was drawn and pinched, and his eyes showed the fear that was upon him. When he stood before the murdered man, he shook like a leaf in the wind, put his face in his hands, and burst into tears.

"I didn't do it, friends," he cried. "On my honour I never did it!"

"Who has accused you?" shouted a voice.

These words had their effect. Potter lifted his face and looked

around him with a sad hopelessness in his eyes. He saw Injun Joe, and called to him: "Oh, Joe, Joe! You promised me that you'd never . . ."

"Is that your knife?" and it was held before him by the Sheriff.

Potter would have fallen if they had not caught him and lowered him to the ground. Then he said, in a broken voice:

"Tell them, Joe—it's no use any more."

Joe began to speak, telling how Muff Potter had murdered the young doctor. Huckleberry and Tom stood dumb and staring and heard the hard-hearted liar make his statement, quite convinced that he had sold himself to the devil. He had now become to them the most dreadful object they had ever looked upon, and they could not take their eyes from his face.

He even helped to raise the body of the murdered man and put it in a cart for removal; then stood and watched the Sheriff lead Muff Potter away to the little brick jail that stood at the end of the village . . .

*   *   *   *   *   *   *

Tom's dreadful secret weighed heavily upon his conscience and disturbed his sleep for as much as a week after this; and at breakfast one morning, Sid said:

"Tom, you talk in your sleep so much you keep me awake half the night."

Tom turned pale and dropped his eyes.

"It's a bad sign," said Aunt Polly. "What have you got on your mind, Tom?"

"Nothing. Nothing that I know of." But the boy's hand shook so that he spilled his coffee.

"And you do talk such stuff," Sid went on.

"Last night you said, 'It's blood, that's what it is!' You said that

over and over. And you said, 'Don't worry me so—I'll tell.' Tell what? What is it you'll tell?"

Everything was swimming before Tom now, but Aunt Polly came to his relief without knowing it.

"Sh!" she said sharply. "It's that dreadful murder. I dream about it almost every night myself."

Sid seemed satisfied, and Tom got out of the house as quickly as he could.

Every day or two during this time of sorrow, Tom watched his opportunity and went to the little jail window and handed such small comforts through to the "murderer" as he could get hold of. Injun Joe, meanwhile, had made a statement telling of the fight, without confessing the grave-robbery that had gone before it, and everyone in the little town knew that Muff Potter would surely be condemned to hang for the murder of the poor young doctor.

Then Tom's mind found a new and weighty matter to interest itself about. Becky Thatcher stopped coming to school. Tom had struggled with his pride for a few days, then tried to win her for himself again, but failed to get her to so much as look at him. Now she was ill and he began to find himself hanging round her father's house at nights, feeling very miserable. She was sick. What if she should die! There was horror in the thought.

Next morning he reached school ahead of time. It was noticed that this strange thing had occurred every day of late. And now he hung about the gate of the school-yard instead of playing with his friends. He was sick, he said; and he looked it. He tried to seem to be looking everywhere but where he was really looking—down the road. Tom watched and watched, hoping whenever a bright dress came in sight, and hating the owner of it as

soon as he saw she was not the right one. At last no more dresses appeared, and he entered the empty school-house and sat down to suffer. Then one more dress passed in at the gate, and Tom's heart gave a great bound. The next instant he was out, shouting, laughing, chasing boys, jumping over the fence at risk of life and limb, and keeping a secret eye out all the time to see if Becky Thatcher was noticing. But she seemed to be unconscious of it all; she never looked. He ran towards her, snatched a boy's cap, threw it to the roof of the school-house, broke through a group of boys and fell to the ground under Becky's nose—and she turned with her nose in the air and he heard her say, "My! some people think they're very smart—always showing off!"

Tom's cheeks burned. He gathered himself up and moved off, determined that he would show Becky Thatcher a thing or two. She would see that he could be as independent as some other people. He had no idea then how fast Becky herself was nearing serious trouble....

The master, Mr. Dobbins, had reached middle age with an unsatisfied ambition. He wanted, above all things, to be a doctor. Every day he took a mysterious book out of his desk, and absorbed himself in it at times when no classes occupied his attention. He kept that book under lock and key. Every child in the school was dying to take a look at it, but the chance never came.

That same day it happened that Becky returned early after the noon break. She went into the empty school-room and, as she was passing by the master's desk, she noticed that the key was in the lock! It was a precious moment. She glanced around, found herself alone, and the next instant she had the book in her hands. The title-page carried no information to her mind, so she be-

gan to to turn the leaves. She came at once upon a coloured picture—a human figure. At that moment a shadow fell on the page, and Tom Sawyer stepped in at the door. Becky snatched at the book to close it, and had the hard luck to tear the pictured page half down the middle. She put the book back in the desk, turned the key, and burst out crying with shame and fright:

"Tom Sawyer, you are as mean as you can be, to creep up on a person and look at what they're looking at."

"How could I know you were looking at anything?"

"You ought to be ashamed of yourself. You know you're going to tell on me; and, oh, what shall I do? I'll be whipped, and I never was whipped in school."

Then she stamped her little foot and said:

"*Be* so mean if you want to! Horrible, *horrible* boy!"—and she ran out of the school with a new explosion of crying.

Tom stood still, rather astonished at this behaviour. Presently he said to himself:

"What a curious kind of a fool a girl is. Never been whipped in school! Huh! What's a whipping? Just like a girl—they're so thin-skinned and chicken-hearted. *I'm* not going to tell old Dobbins about the little fool...."

He joined the crowd of shouting boys outside. In a few moments the master arrived and called them all in. Tom did not feel a strong interest in his studies. Every time he stole a glance at the girls' side of the room, Becky's face troubled him, and his heart was filled with pity for her.

A whole hour went by. At last Mr. Dobbins straightened himself up, unlocked his desk, and reached for his book. Most of the pupils only glanced up, but there were two among them that watched his movements with worried eyes. Tom shot a glance

at Becky. He had seen a hunted and helpless rabbit, with a gun levelled at its head, look as she did. Instantly he forgot his quarrel with her. Quick, something must be done!

The master opened the book. There was no hope for Becky now, Tom knew. The next moment the master faced the school. Every eye sank under his look, for there was that in it which filled even the innocent with fear. There was silence while one might count ten; the master was gathering his anger. Then he spoke:

"Who tore this book?"

There was not a sound. One could have heard a pin drop. The stillness continued. The master searched face after face for signs of guilt.

"Benjamin Rogers, did you tear this book?"

"No, sir."

"Joseph Harper, did you?"

It was denied again. The master went through the ranks of boys, considered a while, then turned to the girls:

"Amy Lawrence?"

A shake of the head.

"Gracie Miller?"

The same sign. The next girl was Becky Thatcher. Tom was trembling from head to foot with excitement.

"Rebecca Thatcher?"

Tom glanced at her face; it was white with terror. A thought shot like lightning through his brain. He sprang to his feet and shouted:

"I did it!"

The school stared open-mouthed at this plain confession to so awful a crime; but when Tom stepped forward for his punish-

ment the surprise, the gratitude, the love that shone upon him out of poor Becky's eyes seemed reward enough for a hundred thrashings. He took without a sound the most cruel beating that even Mr. Dobbins had ever given; and also received calmly the added cruelty of a command to remain two hours after school should be dismissed—for he knew who would wait for him outside . . .

Tom went to bed that night happier than he had been for days, and he fell asleep at last with Becky's words ringing in his ears:

"Tom, how *could* you be so noble!"

Chapter Nine
The Trial

The days passed and at last the sleepy summer atmosphere was stirred, and vigorously. The murder trial came on in the court. Immediately it became the most absorbing subject of village talk. Tom could not get away from it. Every reference to the murder sent a cold shiver right through him. He took Huck to a lonely place to have a talk with him.

"Huck, have you ever told anybody about you know what?"

"Why, Tom Sawyer, we wouldn't be alive two days if that got found out. You know that."

Tom nodded.

"I'm tired of all the talk," Huck went on. "It's just Muff Potter, all the time. It makes me want to hide, away from it all."

"I think he's a dead man. Don't you feel sorry for him sometimes?"

"Yes—all the time. He's never done anything to hurt anybody; He's kind of good, really—he gave me half a fish, once, when there wasn't enough for two."

"I know. He's mended my kite, and done things for me, too, Huck. I wish we could get him out of there."

"My! we couldn't get him out, Tom. And they'd only catch him again if we did."

The boys had a long talk, but it brought them little comfort. When night drew on, they did as they had often done before— went to the jail window and gave Potter some tobacco and matches. He was held on the ground floor, and there were no guards to stop them.

His gratitude for their gifts hurt their consciences more than ever before.

"You've been very good to me, boys— better than anybody else in this town. You've good friendly faces, good friendly faces. Get up on one another's backs, and let me shake your hands. That's it—yours will come through the bars, but mine's too big. Little hands, and weak—but they've helped Muff Potter a lot, and they'd help him more if they could."

Tom went home miserable, and his dreams that night were full of horrors. The next day and the day after, he hung about the court-room, waiting for news. Huck was having the same experience, though they were at pains to avoid each other. At the end of the second day the village talk was to the effect that Injun Joe's evidence stood firm and unshaken, and that there was not the slightest question as to what the jury's verdict would be.

Tom was out late that night, and came to bed through the window. He was in a state of great excitement. It was hours

before he got to sleep. All the village flocked to the court-house the next morning, for this was to be the great day.

The trial continued. Every detail of the damaging circumstances which had occurred in the graveyard that morning which all present remembered so well was brought out by the Counsel for the prosecution. He concluded his address by saying:

"The oaths of citizens whose simple word is above suspicion have fastened this awful crime beyond all possibility of doubt upon the unhappy prisoner before us. We rest our case here."

A groan escaped poor Potter, and he put his face in his hands, while a painful silence hung over the court-room. Counsel for the defence rose and said:

"Your Honour, in our remarks at the opening of this trial, we set out to prove that our client did this terrible deed while under the influence of drink. We have changed our mind; we shall not offer that plea. "Then to the clerk: "Call Thomas Sawyer."

A look of astonishment awoke in every face in the house— including Muff Potter's. Every eye fastened itself with wondering interest upon Tom as he rose and took his place upon the stand. The boy looked wild enough, for he was badly scared. He took the oath . . .

"Thomas Sawyer, where were you on the seventeenth of June about the hour of midnight?"

Tom glanced at Injun Joe's face, and his tongue failed him. The audience listened breathless, but the words refused to come. After a few moments, however, the boy got a little of his strength back, and managed to put enough of it into his voice to make himself heard:

"In the graveyard!"

A scornful smile passed across Injun Joe's face.

"Were you anywhere near Horse Williams's grave?"

"Yes, sir."

"How near were you?"

"Near as I am to you."

"Were you hidden or not?"

"I was hidden."

"Where?"

"Behind the elms that grow on the edge of the grave."

Injun Joe gave a sudden start that escaped all eyes but Tom's.

"Anyone with you?"

"Yes, sir. I went there with—"

"Wait—wait a moment. Never mind mentioning your com
panion's name. We will produce him at the proper time. Did
you carry anything there with you?"

Tom hesitated and looked confused. "Only a—a—dead cat."

There was a burst of laughter, which the court checked.

"We will produce the skeleton of that cat. Now, my boy, tell us
everything that occurred —tell it in your own way—don't miss
anything, and don't be afraid."

Tom began, full of hesitation at first, but gaining confidence as
he went along. In a little while every sound stopped but that of
his own voice; every eye fixed itself upon him; the audience hung
upon his words, taking no note of time, lost in the wonder of the
tale. At last Tom began to conclude his story:

"And as the doctor fetched the board around and Muff Potter
fell, Injun Joe jumped with the knife and—"

Crash! Quick as lightning, Injun Joe sprang for a window, tore
his way through all who tried to stop him, and was gone!

What a hero Tom was now! He was the pet of the old, the envy
of the young. His name even went into print, for the village

paper glorified him. There were some who believed that he would be President yet—if he escaped hanging.

As usual, the world was ready to turn right round and make a great deal of fuss of Muff Potter. Now it praised him as happily as it had abused him before.

Tom's days were days of joy, but his nights were seasons of horror. Injun Joe haunted all his dreams, and always with the threat of sudden death in his eye. Poor Huck was in the same state of terror, for Tom had told the whole story to the lawyer the night before the great day of the trial, and Huck was afraid that his share of the business might yet be made public. The poor fellow had got the lawyer to promise secrecy, but what of that? Since Tom's conscience had managed to drive him to the lawyer's house by night, Huck had only the smallest faith in human promises. Daily, Muff Potter's gratitude made Tom glad he had spoken; but each night he wished he had sealed up his tongue. Half the time Tom was afraid Injun Joe would never be captured; the other half he was afraid he would be. He felt sure he could never draw a safe breath again until that man was dead and he had seen the body.

Rewards had been offered, the surrounding country searched but no Injun Joe was found.

The days went by, and each left behind it a slightly lightened weight of fear and anxiety.

Chapter Ten
The Haunted House

There comes a time in every boy's life when he has a desire to go and dig for treasure. This desire came suddenly upon Tom one day. He found Huck Finn and broached the matter to him confidentially. Huck eager to make a start.

"Where shall we dig?" he asked.

"The haunted house of course."

Huck looked worried.

"I don't like haunted houses, Tom," he said. "Why, they're a lot worse than dead people. I couldn't stand such a thing."

"Yes; but, Huck, ghosts only travel around at night—they won't stop us digging there in the daytime."

"Well, that's so. But you know very well people don't go about that haunted house in the day or the night."

"That's because they don't like to go where a man's been murdered, anyway. But nothing's really ever been seen around that house in the night—just some blue light slipping by the window—no regular ghosts."

On Saturday, shortly after noon, the boys approached the haunted house, armed with an old rusty pick and a shovel. When they reached the place, there was something about the dead silence that reigned there under the hot sun, that made them afraid for a moment to go inside. Then they crept to the door and took a trembling peep. They saw a weed-grown, floorless room, an ancient fireplace, vacant windows, a ruined staircase.

They entered softly, talking in whispers, ears straining for the slightest sound, and ready for instant flight.

In a little while familiarity drove away their fears, and they gave the place a critical and interested examination. Next they wanted to look upstairs, so they threw their tools into a corner and up they went. In the corner of one room they found a cupboard that promised mystery, but there was nothing in it. They were about to go down and begin work when:

"Sh!" said Tom, a finger to his lips.

"What is it?" whispered Huck, turning white with fright.

" *Sh!* There! Hear it?"

"Yes! Oh, my! Keep still! They're coming right up the path towards the door!"

The boys stretched themselves out on the floor with their eyes to holes in the boards, and lay waiting in a misery of fear. Two men entered the room below. Each boy said to himself:

"There's the old deaf and dumb Spaniard that's been about town once or twice lately— never saw the other man before."

The other man was a ragged dirty creature, with nothing very pleasant in his face. The Spaniard was wrapped in a coloured blanket; he had a thick white beard, long white hair flowed from under his wide hat, and he wore green goggles. When they came in the other man was talking in a low voice; they sat down on the ground, and the speaker continued his remarks.

"No," he said, "I've thought it over, and I don't like it. It's dangerous."

"Dangerous!" cried the "deaf and dumb" Spaniard, to the great surprise of the boys. "Rubbish!"

This voice made the boys shake in their shoes. It was Injun Joe's. After a long and thoughtful silence, the half-breed said:

"Look here, you go back up the river where you belong. Wait there till you hear from me. We'll do that 'dangerous' job after I've looked around a little and think things look well for it. Then for Texas! We'll travel together."

This was satisfactory. Both men began to yawn, and Injun Joe said:

"I'm dead for want of sleep! It's your turn to watch."

He curled down in the weeds and was soon asleep. His comrade stirred once or twice, and then his head dropped lower and lower.

The boys drew a long grateful breath.

"Now's our chance—come!" whispered Tom.

Huck said: "I can't—I'd die if they were to wake."

Tom urged—Huck held back. They lay there counting the dragging moments; and then they were grateful to note that at last the sun was setting.

Injun Joe sat up, stirred his comrade with his foot and said:

"Here! You're a fine watchman! Nearly time for us to be moving. What'll we do with the money?"

"Leave it here as we've always done, I reckon. Six hundred and fifty dollars in silver's something to carry."

"Well, all right—but it's not in such a very good hiding-place. We'll bury it—and bury it deep."

"Good idea," said the comrade, who walked across the room, knelt down, raised one of the hearth-stones and took out a bag that jingled pleasantly. He took from it twenty or thirty dollars for himself and as much for Injun Joe. Then he passed the bag to the latter, who was on his knees in the corner now, digging with his knife.

The boys forgot all their fears in an instant. They watched

every movement. Luck! It was beyond all imagination! Six hundred dollars was money enough to make half a dozen boys rich!

Joe's knife struck upon something.

"What is it?" said his comrade.

"It's a box, I believe. Here, lend a hand, and we'll see what it's here for. Never mind, I've knocked a hole in it."

He reached his hand in and drew it out again.

"Man, it's money!"

The two men examined the handful of coins. They were gold! The boys above were as excited as themselves.

Joe's comrade said: "We'll make quick work of this. There's an old rusty pick over among the weeds in the corner—I saw it a minute ago."

He ran and brought the boys' pick and shovel. Joe took the pick, looked it over critically, shook his head, then began to use it.

The box was soon pulled out. It was not very large; it was iron-bound and had been very strong before the slow years had injured it.

"Pardner, there's thousands of dollars there," said Injun Joe.

"It was always said that Murrel's gang was around here one summer," the stranger observed.

"This makes it look like it," said Injun Joe.

"Now you won't need to do that job."

"You don't know me," Joe replied. "It's not robbery altogether—it's revenge!" A wicked light flamed in his eyes. "Go back to your place, and stand by till you hear from me."

"Well, if you say so. What'll we do with this bury it again?"

"Yes." (Great delight overhead.) "No! That pick had fresh earth on it!" (The boys were sick with terror in a moment.) "Who

brought it—and where have they gone? Have you heard anybody—seen anybody? What!

Bury it again and leave them to come and see the ground disturbed? Not likely! We'll take it to my den."

"Why, of course! You mean number one?"

"No—number two—under the cross."

"All right. It's nearly dark enough to start."

Injun Joe got up and went about from window to window, cautiously peeping out. Presently he said:

"Who could have brought those tools here? Do you reckon they can be upstairs?"

The boys almost died of fright. Joe put his hand on his knife and turned towards the stairway. The boys could hear his step on the boards. They were about to spring for the cupboard, when there was a crash of rotten wood. Injun Joe landed on the ground among the ruins of the stairway. He picked himself up cursing, and his comrade said:

"Now, what's the use of all that? If it's anybody, and they're up there, let them stay there—who cares? It will be dark in fifteen minutes—and then let them follow us if they want to. In my opinion, whoever brought these things in here caught a sight of us, and took us for ghosts or devils or something. I'll bet they're running yet."

Joe was persuaded. Shortly afterwards the pair slipped out of the house in the gathering darkness, and moved towards the river with their precious box.

Tom and Huck rose up, weak but greatly relieved, and made haste to reach the ground again and take the track over the hill. Follow? Not they. They decided to keep a look-out for the Spaniard when he should come to town, and follow him to "number

two", wherever that might be. Then a terrible thought occurred to Tom.

"Revenge? What if he means us, Huck?"

"Oh, don't," said Huck, nearly fainting.

They talked it all over, and as they entered town they agreed to believe that he might possibly mean somebody else—at least that he might mean nobody but Tom, since only Tom had appeared against him in court.

Very, very small comfort it was to Tom to be alone in danger! To have company would be a great improvement, he thought.

His dreams that night again were troubled ones. Four times he had his hands on that rich treasure, and four times it wasted to nothing in his fingers. In the morning, he snatched a hurried breakfast and went off to find Huck.

"Huck," he said, in a determined voice, "we've got to track down that money."

"Tom, we'll never find Injun Joe. I'd feel shaky if I saw him, anyway."

"So would I; but I'd like to see him anyway, and track him to his number two. What do you reckon it is?"

"I don't know. Let me think a minute. Here—it's the number of a room—in a tavern, you know!"

"Yes! I'm sure that's it! There are only two taverns. We can find out easily. You wait here till I come back."

Tom was off at once. He was gone half an hour. He found that, in one of the town's taverns, room number two was a mystery. The tavern-keeper's young son said it was kept locked all the time, and he never saw anybody go into it or come out of it except at night. He had made the most of the mystery by entertaining himself with the idea that the room was haunted. And

he had noticed that there was a light in there the night before.

"I reckon that's the number two we're after," said Tom excitedly. "I'll tell you what, Huck. The back door of that number two is the door that comes out into that little alley between the tavern and the brick-store. Now, you get hold of all the door-keys you can find and I'll take all of auntie's, and the first dark night we'll go there and try them. And mind you keep a look-out for Injun Joe, because he said he was going to drop into town and look round for one more chance to get his revenge. If you see him, you just follow him; if he doesn't go to that number two, then it's not the place we want."

"Lordy, I don't want to follow him by myself!"

"Why, it will be night, for sure. He won't ever see you. Remember, he might have found out he couldn't get his revenge, and be going right after that money."

"You're right, Tom. I'll follow him; will, you'll see."

"Now you're talking! Don't you ever weaken, Huck, and I won't."

Chapter Eleven
Night on the Hill

That night Tom and Huck were ready for their adventure. They hung about the neighbourhood of the tavern till after nine, one watching the alley at a distance and the other the tavern door. Nobody entered the alley or left it. The night promised to be a fair one. Tom went home, on the understanding that if some degree of darkness came on, Huck was to come and "meow".

But the night remained clear, and Huck gave up watching and retired to bed in an empty sugar barrel about twelve.

Tuesday the boys had the same ill-luck. Also Wednesday. But Thursday night promised better. Tom slipped out with his aunt's old tin lantern, and a large towel with which to blindfold it. He hid the lantern in Huck's sugar barrel and the watch began. Time passed: there was no sign of the Spaniard.

Tom got his lantern, lit it in the barrel, wrapped it in the towel, and the two boys crept towards the tavern. Huck stood guard and Tom felt his way into the alley.

For Huck there was a season of waiting anxiety. It seemed hours since Tom had vanished. Huck feared all sorts of things, but suddenly there was a flash of light, and Tom came tearing by him.

"Run!" he said. "Run for your life!"

He needn't have repeated it. Huck was making thirty or forty miles an hour in about two seconds. The boys never stopped till they reached the other end of the village. As soon as Tom got his breath he said:

"Huck, it was awful! I tried all those keys, but they wouldn't fit the lock. Well, without noticing what I was doing, I took hold of the knob, and open comes the door! It wasn't locked! I crept in and shook off the towel, and—Huck!—I almost stepped on Injun Joe's hand!"

Huck's eyes almost fell out of his head. "No!" he said.

"Yes. He was asleep on the floor with his arms spread out. Drunk, I reckon. I just turned and started out the door—"

"Did you see that box?"

"Huck, I didn't wait to look around. I didn't see the box, I didn't see any cross and I'm not going in there again till we know Injun Joe's not there. Now if we watch every night, we'll

be sure to see him go out some time or other, then we'll snatch that box quicker than lightning."

"Well, I'm agreed. I'll watch the whole night long—and sleep in the daytime."

"That's it," Tom agreed. "Any time you see something's up in the night, just run round to my house and meow."

The first thing Tom heard on Friday morning was a glad piece of news—Becky Thatcher had persuaded her mother to appoint the next day for a picnic for all her school friends. The invitations were sent out before sunset, and the young people of the village were thrown into a fever of preparation. Tom's excitement helped to keep him awake until a late hour. He had good hopes of hearing Huck's "meow" and having his treasure to astonish Becky and his friends with next day. But he was disappointed. No signal came that night.

By ten o'clock next morning a gay and happy company was gathered at the Thatcher's house. The children were considered safe enough under the wings of a few young ladies of eighteen and a few young gentlemen of twenty or so. The old steam ferryboat had been hired for the occasion: and soon the happy party moved along the main street carrying the foodbaskets. The last thing Mrs. Thatcher said to Becky was:

"You'll not get back till late. Perhaps you'd better stay all night with some of the girls that live near the ferry landing, child."

"Then I'll stay with Susy Harper, mother."

"Very well—and mind you behave yourself"

Presently, as they walked along, Tom said to Becky:

"I'll tell you what we'll do. Instead of staying with the Harper's we'll climb right up the hill and stop at Widow Douglas's. She'll have ice-cream! And she'll be glad to have us."

Becky thought for a moment, and said:

"What will mother say?"

"She won't know," answered Tom simply. "In fact, I'll bet she would have said to go there if she'd thought of it. I know she would!"

Becky was persuaded, and it was decided to say nothing to anybody about the night's programme. It occurred to Tom that perhaps Huck might come this very night and give the signal. Still, he could not bear to give up the fun at Widow Douglas's. And why should he give it up—the signal had not come the night before, so why should it be any more likely to come to-night?

Three miles below town the ferryboat stopped at the mouth of a wooded hollow and tied up. The crowd were soon ashore and in no time the forest distances echoed with shouts and laughter. After the games, came the feast, and when everyone had eaten his fill, somebody shouted: "Who's ready for the cave?"

Everybody was. Bundles of candles were produced, and everyone rushed for the entrance to the great cave. Its thick oak door stood ready open. The procession went filing down the main avenue, with the light from dozens of candles showing the high walls of rock on both sides. Every few steps other and more narrow avenues branched off from it on either hand, for McDougal's cave was a labyrinth of passages and paths that ran into each other and out again and led nowhere. It was said that one might wander days and nights together and never find the end of the cave. No man "knew" the cave. That was an impossible thing. Most of the young men knew a part of it, and it was not usual to go beyond this known section. Tom Sawyer knew as much of the cave as anyone.

The procession moved along the main avenue some three-quarters of a mile, and then groups and couples began to slip aside into branch avenues. Parties were able to hide from each other for the space of half an hour without going beyond the "known" ground.

By-and-by, one group after another returned to the mouth of the cave, all entirely delighted with the success of the day. Most of them were astonished to find that night was now at hand, and all made haste to board the ferryboat, which was soon under way.

Huck was already upon his watch when the lights of the boat moved by upon the river. He wondered what boat it was—and then put all his attention upon his business. The night was growing cloudy and dark. Eleven o'clock came. Darkness everywhere now. Huck waited what seemed a weary long time, but nothing happened. Why not give it up and go to sleep, he thought?

A noise fell upon his ear. He was all attention in an instant. The alley door closed softly. The next moment two men brushed by him, and one seemed to have something under his arm. It must be that box! So they were going to remove the treasure. Why call Tom now? The men would get away with the box and never be found again. No, he would follow them by himself.

They moved up the river street, and took a path that led up Cardiff Hill. Half-way up the hill they passed by the old Welshman's place, and still climbed upward. The path narrowed and wound between high bushes, and they vanished in the darkness. Huck closed up now, for they would never be able to see him. He moved on a little, then stopped altogether; listened; no sound; none, save the beating of his own heart. Had he lost them? He was about to spring forward when a man cleared his throat, not

four feet from him! Now there was a low voice—a very low voice—Injun Joe's:

"There's lights in the house late as it is. She must have company, curse her!"

Huck went cold all over—this, then, was the "revenge" job! His thought was to fly. Then he remembered that the Widow Douglas had been kind to him more than once, and perhaps these men were going to murder her.

"Yes—there is company there, I reckon. You'd better give it up."

This was that stranger's voice—the stranger of the haunted house.

"Give it up, when I'm leaving this country for ever! I've told you before, her husband was rough on me—he had me jailed—and he had me whipped, with all the town looking on! Now I'll take it out of her!"

"Oh, don't kill her! Don't do that!"

"Kill? Who said anything about killing? When you want to get revenge on a woman you don't kill her—you spoil her good looks. You slit her nose—you cut off an ear—"

Huck was already moving back. A twig broke under his foot. His breath stopped and he listened. Injun Joe was still talking. Huck turned and stepped quickly but cautiously along. When he felt quite safe, he ran as fast as he could down the hill till he reached the Welshman's. He banged at the door, and presently the heads of the old man and his two big sons were put out of the windows.

"Who's banging? What do you want?"

"It's Huckleberry Finn. Let me in—quick! I'll tell everything."

"Let him in, lads," said the old Welshman, "and let's see what

the trouble is."

"Please don't ever tell I told you," were Huck's first words when he got in." I'd be killed for sure—but the widow's been a good friend to me, and I want to tell."

"Out with it," ordered the old Welshman, "and nobody here will ever tell, lad."

Three minutes later the old man and his sons, well-armed, were up the hill and creeping along the path that led to the Widow Douglas's. Huck went no further. He hid behind a rock and fell to listening. There was a long, anxious silence, and then all of a sudden there was an explosion of guns and a cry. Huck waited for no more. He sprang away and down the hill as fast as his legs would carry him.

Chapter Twelve
The Dreadful Discovery

As the earliest suspicion of dawn appeared on Sunday morning, Huck felt his way up the hill and knocked at the old Welshman's door. In a moment, a call came from a window:

"Who's there?"

"Do please let me in. It's only Huck Finn."

"It's a name that can open this door at any time. You're welcome, lad!"

These were strange words to the orphan boy's ears. He was taken in and given a seat, and the old man and his tall sons dressed with all speed.

"Now, my boy, I hope you're good and hungry because break-

fast will soon be ready. I and the boys hoped you'd turn up and stop here last night."

"I was awful scared," said Huck. "I started running when the guns went off, and I didn't stop for three miles. Are those two dead?"

"No, they're not—I'm sorry to say. We crept along the path till we got within fifteen feet of them—and just then I found I was going to sneeze. I was in the lead, and when the sneeze started those two wretches ran to get out of the path. I called out 'Fire, boys!' and we all fired ahead of us. But they were off in a flash, and we after them, down through the woods. When we lost the sound of their feet, we gave up the chase, and went down and called the Sheriff. As soon as it's light the Sheriff and a gang are going to search the woods. I wish we had some sort of description of those two—it would help a good deal. But you couldn't see what they were like in the dark, I suppose?"

"Oh, yes, I saw them down town, and followed them. One's the old deaf and dumb Spaniard that's been around here once or twice." Huck looked into the old man's honest eyes a moment, and then bent over and whispered in his ear. "It isn't a Spaniard, though—it's Injun Joe!"

The old man almost jumped out of his chair. In a moment he said: "It's all plain enough now. When you talked about slitting noses, I thought that perhaps that was something you'd just made up yourself—but that's just the sort of thing we can expect from Injun Joe."

During breakfast the talk went on. The old man said that the last thing he had done before going to bed was to get a lantern and search the path where Injun Joe and the stranger had waited. He had found a bundle of—

" Of *what?*"

The words leaped like lightning from Huck's lips. His eyes were staring wide, and he had stopped breathing—waiting for the answer. The Welshman started—stared in return— then replied

"Of robber's tools."

Huck sank back, deeply grateful, for he had feared that the bundle might contain the treasure which he looked upon as belonging to Tom and himself. Now, he decided, the treasure must still be in number two. The men would be captured and jailed that day, and he and Tom could seize the gold that night without any fear of trouble or interruption.

The old Welshman said: "Poor old chap, you look white and tired. I'm going to put you to bed here a good sleep will do you a lot of good."

Just as breakfast was completed there was a knock at the door. Huck jumped for a hiding-place, while the Welshman admitted several ladies and gentlemen, among them the Widow Douglas.

The Welshman had to tell the story of the night to the visitors. The widow was full of gratitude.

"There's another that you should be more grateful to than me and my boys," the Welsh man told her, "but he won't allow me to mention his name. We wouldn't ever have been there but for him."

Of course this excited a great deal of curiosity, but the Welshman refused to part with his secret. More visitors came, and the story had to be told and retold for a couple of hours more.

Everybody was early at church that morning. News came that not a sign of the robbers had been yet discovered. When the service was over, Mrs. Thatcher dropped alongside of Mrs. Harper as she moved out of church, and said:

"Is my Becky going to sleep all day at your house?"

"Your Becky?"

"Yes," with a surprised look. "Didn't she stay with you last night?"

"Why, no."

Mrs. Thatcher turned pale and sank into a seat just as Aunt Polly passed by. Aunt Polly said:

"Good morning, Mrs. Thatcher. I suppose my Tom stayed at your house last night—one of you. And now he's afraid to come to church. I've got to settle with him."

Mrs. Thatcher shook her head and turned paler than ever.

"He didn't stay with us," said Mrs. Harper. A marked anxiety came into Aunt Polly's face.

"Joe Harper, have you seen my Tom this morning?"

"No, I haven't."

"When did you see him last?"

Joe tried to remember, but was not sure he could say. The people had stopped moving out of church. Children were anxiously questioned, and young teachers. They all said they had not noticed whether Tom and Becky were on board the ferryboat on the way home; it was dark; no one had thought to inquire if anyone was missing. One young man at last spoke his open fear that they were still in the cave. Mrs. Thatcher fainted; Aunt Polly fell to crying.

The alarm passed from lip to lip, from group to group, from street to street; and within five minutes the bells were ringing wildly, and the whole town seemed to be on the move. The robbers were forgotten, horses were saddled, boats were manned and before the horror was half an hour old two hundred men were pouring down the high road and river toward the cave.

All the long afternoon the village seemed empty and dead

Many women visited Aunt Polly and Mrs. Thatcher, and tried to comfort them.

All night the town waited for news; but when morning dawned at last, all the word that came was, "Send more candles, and send food."

The old Welshman came home towards daylight. He found Huck still in the bed that had been provided for him, very ill with fever. The doctors were all at the cave, so the Widow Douglas came and took charge of the sick boy.

Three dreadful days and nights dragged their slow hours along, and when that time had passed there were not many left who had hope enough, or strength enough, to go on searching for the missing boy and girl.

Chapter Thirteen
The Escape

Now to return to Tom and Becky's share in the picnic. They wandered along the familiar passages of the cave with the rest of the company, and then turned down a side-avenue by themselves, holding their candles high and reading the names, dates, and addresses which had been scratched upon the rocky walls. Presently they came to a place where a little stream of water fell over a ledge to make a waterfall. Tom squeezed his small body behind it in order to light it for Becky's benefit. He found that it curtained a sort of steep natural stairway between narrow walls, and at once the ambition to be an explorer seized him. Becky was eager to follow, and they wound this way and that far down

into the secret depths of the cave, searching for wonders to tell the upper world about. Passage after passage was left behind them until Tom found an underground lake, which stretched away until its shape was lost in the shadows. Now for the first time the children noticed the deep stillness of the place. Becky said:

"It seems a long time since we heard any of the others. We'd better start back."

"Yes," said Tom, "perhaps we'd better."

They started through a passage and went in silence a long way, glancing at each new opening to see if there was anything familiar about it; but the openings were all strange. Each time Tom made an examination, he said:

"Oh, it's all right. This isn't the one, but we'll come to it soon."

At last even he felt a little dread at his heart, while Becky tried hard to keep back her tears.

Tom stopped.

"Listen!" he said.

Silence; silence so deep that even their breathing sounded loud and heavy. Tom shouted. Echoes were the only answer.

"Tom," cried Becky, "we're lost! I know it! We'll never get out of this awful place! Oh, why did we ever leave the others?"

She sank to the ground, and cried in such a heart-broken manner that Tom was scared that she might die or lose her reason. He sat down by her and put his arms around her, begging her to be brave. She said she would try to hope again, she would get up and follow wherever he might lead, and so they moved on again—all they could do was to move, keep moving.

After a while, Tom took Becky's candle and blew it out. Becky understood, and her hope died again. She knew that Tom had

a whole candle and three or four pieces in his pocket— yet he must be careful with them.

A long time after this Tom said that they must try to find a stream. They found one presently and Tom said it was time to rest. They sat down, and Tom fastened his candle to the wall in front of them with some clay.

By-and-by Becky suggested that they move on again. Tom was silent for a moment. Then he said:

"Becky, can you bear it if I tell you something?"

Becky's face paled, but she said she thought she could.

"Well then, we must stay here, where there's water to drink. That little piece is our last candle."

"Will they miss us and hunt for us?" asked Becky.

"Yes, they will! Certainly they will!"

"When would they miss us, Tom?"

"When they got back to the boat, I reckon. Anyway, your mother would miss you as soon as they got home."

A frightened look in Becky's face made Tom aware of his blunder. Becky was not to have gone home that night! The children became silent and thoughtful. They fastened their eyes upon their bit of candle, and watched it melt away; saw the feeble flame rise and fall, rise and fall, and then—the horror of absolute blackness reigned.

The weary time dragged on, and hunger came to torture the pair. They slept, and awoke, and drank water, and thought, and slept again, and waited, and listened—but no sound came. Tom believed it must be Tuesday by this time.

At last an idea struck him. There were some side-passages near at hand. It would be better to explore some of these than to bear the weight of the heavy time in idleness. He took a kite-line

from his pocket, tied it to a rock, and he and Becky started off, Tom in the lead, unwinding the line as he felt his way along.

At the end of twenty steps the passage turned. Tom got down on his knees and felt below, and then as far round the corner as he could reach; he made an effort to stretch yet a little farther to the right, and at that moment, not twenty yards away a human hand, holding a candle, appeared from behind a rock. Tom gave a shout of joy, and in an instant that hand was followed by the body to which it belonged —Injun Joe's! Tom stood frozen; he could not move. He was grateful the next moment to see the "Spaniard" take to his heels and get himself out of sight . . .

Tom wondered that Joe had not recognized his shout and come over and killed him, but the echoes must have changed his voice. He made up his mind that if he had strength enough to get back to the stream he would stay there, and that nothing should tempt him to run the risk of meeting Injun Joe again. He did not tell Becky what he had seen. He told her he only shouted "for luck".

Another long wait; another long sleep beside the stream. The children awoke tortured by hunger. Tom proposed to explore another passage, but Becky was very weak. She said she would wait, now, where she was, and die it would not be long.

Tom kissed her and made a show of being confident of finding the searchers or a way of escape from the cave; then he took the kiteline in his hand and went on his hands and knees, feeling before him, down one of the passages, tortured by hunger and sick with the thought of death drawing near . . .

Tuesday afternoon came, and the day faded into night. The lost children had not been found. Public prayers had been offered up for them, and many a private prayer also. Most of the searchers had given up, and gone back to work, saying that it

was plain the children could never be found. The village went to its rest, sad and weary.

In the middle of the night the church bells burst into life, and in a moment the streets were filled with half-dressed people, all calling, "Turn out! turn out! They're found! they're found!"

The population moved towards the river, met the children coming in an open carriage drawn by shouting citizens, flocked round it, joined in the procession, and marched up the village street singing and cheering in their delight.

Nobody went to bed again after that; it was the greatest night the little town had ever seen. During the first half-hour a procession of people filed through the Thatcher house, seized the saved ones and kissed them. The happiness of Aunt Polly and Mrs. Thatcher was complete.

Tom lay back and told the history of the great adventure; and finished with a description of how he followed a passage to the extent of his kite-line, and was about to turn back when he saw a white spot, far-off, that looked like daylight; dropped the line and felt his way towards it, pushed his head and shoulders through a small hole, and saw the river running by!

He told how he went back for Becky and broke the good news, and how she almost died for joy when he had led her to where she could see the daylight; how he pushed his way out of the hole and then helped her out; how some men came along in a boat and how they talked to them while the sun went down; and how the men took them to a house, gave them supper, made them rest for a time, and then brought them home.

Three days and nights of hunger and anxiety were not to be shaken off at once, as Tom and Becky soon discovered. They were in bed all of Wednesday and Thursday, but Tom was down

town on Friday, and as good as ever by Saturday; but Becky did not leave her room until Sunday, and then she looked as if she had passed through a terrible illness.

Tom learned of Huck's illness, but was not admitted to see him until Monday. He was admitted daily after that, but was warned to keep quiet about his adventure and not to talk of anything that was likely to make Huck excited. At home Tom learned that the body of Injun Joe's partner had been found in the river near the ferry landing; he had been drowned while trying to escape perhaps.

About a fortnight after Tom's rescue from the cave he started off to visit Huck, who was now strong enough to hear exciting news—and Tom had some that would interest him, he thought. The Thatcher house was on Tom's way, and he stopped to see Becky. Mr. Thatcher and some friends set Tom talking. Someone asked him if he would like to go to the cave again. Tom said yes, he thought he wouldn't mind it.

Mr. Thatcher said:

"Well, there are others just like you, Tom, no doubt. But we have taken care of that. Nobody will get lost in that cave any more."

"Why?"

"Because I had its big door sealed with iron plates two weeks ago, and three locks put on it; and I've got the keys."

Tom turned as white as a sheet.

"What's the matter boy? Here, run, somebody! Fetch a glass of water!"

The water was brought and thrown into Tom's face.

"Ah, now you're all right. What was the matter with you, Tom?"

"Oh, Mr. Thatcher, Injun Joe's in the cave!"

Chapter Fourteen
The Treasure

When the cave door was unlocked, they found Injun Joe lying stretched upon the ground, dead, with his face close to the crack of the door, as if his eyes had been fixed to the last moment upon the light of the free world outside. Tom was touched, for he knew by his own experience how this wretch had suffered. His pity was moved, but he felt a great sense of relief, and also felt secure for the first time since the day he had lifted his voice against Injun Joe in the court-room.

Injun Joe was buried near the mouth of the cave, and people flocked there in boats and carts for the funeral.

The morning after the funeral, Tom took Huck to a private place to have an important talk. Huck had learned all about Tom's adventure from the Welshman and the Widow Douglas, but Tom said he reckoned there was one thing they had not told him. Huck's face grew sad.

"I know what it is," he said. "You got into number two, but the treasure wasn't there."

"Huck," said Tom seriously, "that money wasn't ever in number two!"

Huck's eyes burned suddenly with a brilliant light.

"What! Tom, have you got on the track of that money again?"

"Huck, it's in the cave! Will you help me get it out?"

"You bet I will—if it's somewhere where we can find our way to, and not get lost."

"We can do that without the least trouble in the world."

"When?"

"Right now—if you feel strong enough."

"Strong enough—let's go, Tom!"

A little after noon the boys borrowed a small boat from a citizen who was absent, and got under way at once. When they were several miles below the cave, Tom said:

"Do you see that white place up on the hill? Well, that's one of my marks. We'll go on shore now.

They landed.

"Now, Huck," said Tom a minute or two later, "from where you're standing you could touch that hole. See if you can find it."

Huck searched all about the place, and found nothing. Tom marched into a thick bunch of bushes and said:

"Here you are! Look at it, Huck—but keep quiet about it. It's my secret, remember."

The boys entered the hole, Tom in the lead. They worked their way to the farther end of the tunnel, then made fast the kite-line they had brought with them and moved on. A few steps brought them to the stream, and Tom felt a cold shiver run through him.

The boys began to whisper now, for the stillness began to weigh heavily upon their spirits. They went on, and presently entered the passage where Tom had seen Injun Joe. The candles showed before them a steep clay hill that dropped down for about twenty feet. Tom whispered:

"Now I'll show you something, Huck."

He held up his candle and said:

"Look as far round the corner as you can. Do you see that?

There—on the rock—marked out with candle smoke."

"Tom, its a *cross!*"

"*Now* where's your number two? '*Under the cross*', eh? This is where I saw Injun Joe lift up his candle, Huck!"

Huck stared at the sign for a moment, and then said: "It's luck for us, that cross is. I reckon we'll climb down there, and have a hunt for the box."

Tom went first, scrambling down through the clay of the hillside. Huck followed. At the bottom, Tom said:

"Look, there's footprints all round this rock. I bet you the money is under it. I'm going to dig in the clay."

"Good idea, Tom," said Huck eagerly.

Tom had dug only four inches when he struck wood. Some boards were soon uncovered and removed. They had hidden a natural hole in the rock. Tom got into this with his candle and discovered a narrow way leading to a little cave.

"My goodness, Huck, look here!"

There was the treasure-box, and two guns in leather cases.

"Got it at last!" said Huck, putting his hand among the golden coins. "My, but we're rich, Tom!"

"Huck, I always reckoned we'd get it. But let's not fool around here. Let's get it out just as quick as we can. Let me see if I can lift the box."

It weighed about fifty pounds. Tom could lift it after an awkward fashion, but could not carry it conveniently.

"I thought so," he said; "they carried it as if it was heavy that day at the haunted house. It's a good thing I thought of bringing the two sacks along."

The money was soon in the bags, and some time later the boys lifted them out of the hole in the bushes. As the sun set, they

pushed off in their boat. Tom rowed along the shore in the gathering darkness, and they landed shortly after dark.

"Now, Huck," said Tom, "we'll hide the money in the widow's wood-shed, and I'll come up in the morning and we'll count it and divide it. Then we'll hunt up a place in the woods for it where it will be safe. Just you lie here and watch the stuff while I run and borrow Benny Taylor's little wagon."

He went off, returned with the wagon, put the two small sacks into it, threw some old rags on top of them, and started off, dragging the wagon behind him. When the boys reached the Welshman's house they stopped to rest. Just as they were about to move on, the Welshman stepped out and said:

"I'm glad I've met you, boys. Now, come along with me—you're keeping everybody waiting. I'll pull the wagon for you. Why, it's not as light as it might be. Got bricks in it, or old metal?"

"Old metal," said Tom.

" I thought so. Now, hurry along, hurry along!"

The boys wanted to know what the hurry was about.

"Never mind. You'll see when we get to Widow Douglas's."

A few minutes later Huck found himself being pushed by Tom into Mrs. Douglas's drawing-room. The Welshman left the wagon near the door and followed.

The place was grandly lighted, and everybody that was of any consequence in the village was there. The Thatchers were there, the Harpers, Aunt Polly, Sid, the minister, the editor of the village newspaper, and a great many more, and all dressed in their best. The widow made the boys welcome, in spite of the fact that they were covered with clay and candle-grease. Aunt Polly shook her head and looked at Tom as if he were a disgrace to her. The Welshman said:

"Tom wasn't at home, so I gave him up; but I met him and Huck right at my door, so I just brought them along in a hurry."

"And you did just right," said the widow. "Come with me, boys."

She took them to a bedroom, and said:

"Now wash and dress yourselves. Here are two new suits of clothes shirts, socks, everything complete. They're Huck's—no, no thanks, Huck—Mr. Jones bought one and I the other. But they'll fit you as well, Tom. Get into them. We'll wait—come down when you are ready."

Then she left.

Huck said: "Tom, we can run away if we can find a rope. The window isn't far from the ground."

"What do you want to run away for?"

"I'm not used to that kind of crowd. I can't stand it. I'm not going down there, Tom."

"Oh, that's nothing, Huck. I don't mind it a bit. I'll take care of you."

Some minutes later two fairly clean—and very uncomfortable boys appeared downstairs. Two minutes later still the widow's guests were at the supper-table, and a dozen children sat at little side-tables in the same room, after the fashion of the country and day. At the proper time Mr. Jones rose and made a little speech, in which he told all about Huck's share in the saving of Widow Douglas from the revenge of Injun Joe. Everybody made a show of being astonished, but it was clear that they already knew about it. The widow heaped so much gratitude upon Huck, that he very nearly forgot the awful feel of his new clothing in the worse feeling of having everybody stare at him and praise him.

The widow said she meant to give Huck a home under her

roof and have him educated; and that when she could spare the money she would start him up in business. Tom's chance was come. He said:

"Huck doesn't need it. Huck's rich!"

Nothing but a heavy strain upon the good manners of the company kept back a laugh at this joke. But the silence was a little awkward. Tom broke it.

"Huck's got money. Perhaps you don't believe it, but he's got lots of it. You just wait a minute."

He ran out of doors. The company looked at each other with a puzzled interest, and then at Huck, who had gone all red in the face.

"I don't know what's got into Tom," said Aunt Polly, and added, with a sigh: "Well, it's hard to make that boy out at any time. I never—"

Tom entered, struggling with the weight of his sacks, and Aunt Polly did not finish her sentence. Tom poured the mass of yellow coins upon the table and said:

"There what did I tell you? Half of it's Huck's, and half of it's mine!"

The spectacle took the general breath away.

All stared; nobody spoke for a moment. Then there was a loud call for an explanation. Tom said he could supply it, and he did. The tale was long, but full of interest. There were no interruptions at all. When he had finished, the Welshman said:

"I thought I had fixed up a little surprise for this occasion, but it doesn't amount to anything now. Tom and Huck have provided the real surprise!"

The money was counted. The sum amounted to a little over twelve thousand dollars. It was more than anyone present had

ever seen at one time before, though several persons were there who owned property worth a great deal more than that.

The reader may rest satisfied that Tom's and Huck's good luck made a great stir in the little village of St. Petersburg. Wherever Tom and Huck appeared they were admired and stared at. The boys were not able to remember that their remarks had possessed much weight before, but now their sayings were treasured and repeated! The village paper even published their life-stories.

The Widow Douglas took care of Huck's money, and Judge Thatcher did the same with Tom's at Aunt Polly's request. Both lads now had an income that seemed to them almost beyond belief a dollar for every week-day in the year and half of the Sundays. A dollar and a quarter a week would board, lodge, and school a boy in those old simple days—and clothe him and wash him too, for that matter.

Judge Thatcher had formed a great opinion of Tom. He said that no ordinary boy would ever have got his daughter out of the cave. He hoped to see Tom a great lawyer or a great soldier some day.

So ends this story. Since it is the history of a boy, it must stop here; the story could not go much further without becoming the history of a man. When an author writes a story about grown people, he knows exactly where to stop—that is, with a marriage; but when he writes of children, he must stop where best he can.

Illustrated Chosen Classics
———— Retold ————

Titles available in this series:

PETER HADDOCK PUBLISHING